# Rhymes of a Rolling Stone

I have no doubt at all the Devil grins,
  As seas of ink I spatter.
Ye gods, forgive my "literary" sins—
  The other kind don't matter.

# Rhymes of a Rolling Stone

### BY

## ROBERT W. SERVICE
Author of "The Spell of the Yukon,"
"Ballads of a Cheechako," etc.

**NEW YORK**
**Dodd, Mead and Company**
1923

# Contents

# CONTENTS

# Rhymes of a Rolling Stone

## PRELUDE

*I* SING no idle songs of dalliance days,
  No dreams Elysian inspire my rhyming;
I have no Celia to enchant my lays,
No pipes of Pan have set my heart to chiming.
I am no wordsmith dripping gems divine
Into the golden chalice of a sonnet;
If love songs witch you, close this book of mine,
  Waste no time on it.

Yet bring I to my work an eager joy,
A lusty love of life and all things human;
Still in me leaps the wonder of the boy,
A pride in man, a deathless faith in woman.
Still red blood calls, still rings the valiant fray;
Adventure beacons through the summer gloaming:
Oh long and long and long will be the day
  Ere I come homing!

## PRELUDE

This earth is ours to love: lute, brush and pen,
They are but tongues to tell of life sincerely;
The thaumaturgic Day, the might of men,
O God of Scribes, grant us to grave them clearly!
Grant heart that homes in heart, then all is well.
Honey is honey-sweet, howe'er the hiving.
Each to his work, his wage at evening bell
      The strength of striving.

## A ROLLING STONE

*THERE'S sunshine in the heart of me,*
*My blood sings in the breeze;*
*The mountains are a part of me,*
*I'm fellow to the trees.*
*My golden youth I'm squandering,*
*Sun-libertine am I;*
*A-wandering, a-wandering,*
*Until the day I die.*

I was once, I declare, a Stone-Age man,
And I roomed in the cool of a cave;
I have known, I will swear, in a new life-span,
The fret and the sweat of a slave:
For far over all that folks hold worth,
There lives and there leaps in me
A love of the lowly things of earth,
And a passion to be free.

To pitch my tent with no prosy plan,
To range and to change at will;
To mock at the mastership of man,
To seek Adventure's thrill.

3

Carefree to be, as a bird that sings;
    To go my own sweet way;
To reck not at all what may befall,
    But to live and to love each day.

To make my body a temple pure
    Wherein I dwell serene;
To care for the things that shall endure,
    The simple, sweet and clean.
To oust out envy and hate and rage,
    To breathe with no alarm;
For Nature shall be my anchorage,
    And none shall do me harm.

To shun all lures that debauch the soul,
    The orgied rites of the rich;
To eat my crust as a rover must
    With the rough-neck down in the ditch.
To trudge by his side whate'er betide;
    To share his fire at night;
To call him friend to the long trail-end,
    And to read his heart aright.

To scorn all strife, and to view all life
    With the curious eyes of a child;
From the plangent sea to the prairie,
    From the slum to the heart of the Wild.

# A ROLLING STONE

From the red-rimmed star to the speck of sand,
    From the vast to the greatly small;
For I know that the whole for good is planned,
    And I want to see it all.

To see it all, the wide world-way,
    From the fig-leaf belt to the Pole;
With never a one to say me nay,
    And none to cramp my soul.
In belly-pinch I will pay the price,
    But God! let me be free;
For once I know in the long ago,
    They made a slave of me.

In a flannel shirt from earth's clean dirt,
    Here, pal, is my calloused hand!
Oh, I love each day as a rover may,
    Nor seek to understand.
To *enjoy* is good enough for me;
    The gipsy of God am I;
Then here's a hail to each flaring dawn!
And here's a cheer to the night that's gone!
And may I go a-roaming on
    Until the day I die!

Then every star shall sing to me
Its song of liberty;
And every morn shall bring to me
Its mandate to be free.
In every throbbing vein of me
I'll feel the vast Earth-call;
O body, heart and brain of me
Praise Him who made it all!

## THE SOLDIER OF FORTUNE

"**D**ENY your God!" they ringed me with their
 spears;
Blood-crazed were they, and reeking from the strife;
Hell-hot their hate, and venom-fanged their sneers,
And one man spat on me and nursed a knife.
And there was I, sore wounded and alone,
I, the last living of my slaughtered band.
Oh sinister the sky, and cold as stone!
In one red laugh of horror reeled the land.
And dazed and desperate I faced their spears,
And like a flame out-leaped that naked knife,
And like a serpent stung their bitter jeers:
" Deny your God, and we will give you life."


Deny my God! Oh life was very sweet!
And it is hard in youth and hope to die;
And there my comrades dear lay at my feet,
And in that blear of blood soon must I lie.
And yet . . . I almost laughed — it seemed so odd,
For long and long had I not vainly tried
To reason out and body forth my God,
And prayed for light, and doubted — and *denied:*
Denied the Being I could not conceive,

7

Denied a life-to-be beyond the grave. . . .
And now they ask me, who do not believe,
Just to deny, to voice my doubt, to save
This life of mine that sings so in the sun,
The bloom of youth yet red upon my cheek,
My only life! — O fools! 'tis easy done,
I will deny . . . and yet I do not speak.


" Deny your God! " their spears are all agleam,
And I can see their eyes with blood-lust shine;
Their snarling voices shrill into a scream,
And, mad to slay, they quiver for the sign.
Deny my God! yes, I could do it well;
Yet if I did, what of my race, my name?
How they would spit on me, these dogs of hell!
Spurn me, and put on me the brand of shame.
A white man's honour! what of that, I say?
Shall these black curs cry " Coward " in my face?
They who would perish for their gods of clay —
Shall I defile my country and my race?
My country! what's my country to me now?
Soldier of Fortune, free and far I roam;
All men are brothers in my heart, I vow;
The wide and wondrous world is all my home.
My country! reverent of her splendid Dead,
Her heroes proud, her martyrs pierced with pain:

For me her puissant blood was vainly shed;
For me her drums of battle beat in vain,
And free I fare, half-heedless of her fate:
No faith, no flag I owe — then why not seek
This last loop-hole of life? Why hesitate?
I will deny . . . and yet I do not speak.


"Deny your God!" their spears are poised on high,
And tense and terrible they wait the word;
And dark and darker glooms the dreary sky,
And in that hush of horror no thing stirred.
Then, through the ringing terror and sheer hate
Leaped there a vision to me — Oh, how far!
A face, Her face . . . through all my stormy fate
A joy, a strength, a glory and a star.
Beneath the pines, where lonely camp-fires gleam,
In seas forlorn, amid the deserts drear,
How I had gladdened to that face of dream!
And never, never had it seemed so dear.
O silken hair that veils the sunny brow!
O eyes of grey, so tender and so true!
O lips of smiling sweetness! must I now
For ever and for ever go from you?
Ah, yes, I must . . . for if I do this thing,
How can I look into your face again?
Knowing you think me more than half a king,
I with my craven heart, my honour slain.

No! no! my mind's made up. I gaze above,
Into that sky insensate as a stone;
Not for my creed, my country, but my Love
Will I stand up and meet my death alone.
Then though it be to utter dark I sink,
The God that dwells in me is not denied;
" Best " triumphs over " Beast,"— and so I think
Humanity itself is glorified. . . .


" And now, my butchers, I embrace my fate.
" Come! let my heart's blood slake the thirsty sod.
" Curst be the life you offer! Glut your hate!
" Strike! Strike, you dogs! I'll *not* deny my God."


I saw the spears that seemed a-leap to slay,
All quiver earthward at the headman's nod;
And in a daze of dream I heard him say:
" Go, set him free who serves so well his God!"

NOW Eddie Malone got a swell grammyfone to
  draw all the trade to his store;
An' sez he: "Come along for a season of song, which
  the like ye had niver before."
Then Dogrib, an' Slave, an' Yellow-knife brave, an' Cree
  in his dinky canoe,
Confluated near, to see an' to hear Ed's grammyfone
  make its dayboo.


Then Ed turned the crank, an' there on the bank they
  squatted like bumps on a log.
For acres around there wasn't a sound, not even the
  howl of a dog.
When out of the horn there sudden was born such a
  marvellous elegant tone;
An' then like a spell on that auddyence fell the voice
  of its first grammyfone.


"*Bad medicine!*" cried Old Tom, the One-eyed, an'
  made for to jump in the lake;
But no one gave heed to his little stampede, so he
  guessed he had made a mistake.

Then Roll-in-the-Mud, a chief of the blood, observed in
    choice Chippewayan:
" You've brought us canned beef, an' it's now my belief
    that this here's a case of ' *canned man.*' "


Well, though I'm not strong on the Dago in song, that
    sure got me goin' for fair.
There was Crusoe an' Scotty, an' Ma'am Shoeman Hank,
    an' Melber an' Bonchy was there.
'Twas silver an' gold, an' sweetness untold to hear all
    them big guinneys sing;
An' thick all around an' inhalin' the sound, them Indians
    formed in a ring.


So solemn they sat, an' they smoked an' they spat, but
    their eyes sort o' glistened an' shone;
Yet niver a word of approvin' occurred till that guy
    Harry Lauder came on.
Then hunter of moose, an' squaw an' papoose jest
    laughed till their stummicks was sore;
Six times Eddie set back that record an' yet they hol-
    lered an' hollered for more.

I'll never forget that frame-up, you bet; them caverns
  of sunset agleam;
Them still peaks aglow, them shadders below, an' the
  lake like a petrified dream;
The teepees that stood by the edge of the wood; the
  evenin' star blinkin' alone;
The peace an' the rest, an' final an' best, the music of
  Ed's grammyfone.

Then sudden an' clear there rang on my ear a song
  mighty simple an' old;
Heart-hungry an' high it thrilled to the sky, all about
  "silver threads in the gold."
'Twas tender to tears, an' it brung back the years, the
  mem'ries that hallow an' yearn;
'Twas home-love an' joy, 'twas the thought of my boy
  . . . an' right there I vowed I'd return.

Big Four-finger Jack was right at my back, an' I saw
  with a kind o' surprise,
He gazed at the lake with a heartful of ache, an' the
  tears irrigated his eyes.
An' sez he: "Cuss me, pard! but that there hits me
  hard; I've a mother does nuthin' but wait.
"She's turned eighty-three, an' she's only got me, an'
  I'm scared it'll soon be too late."

\* \* \* \* \* \* \* \*

# THE GRAMAPHONE AT FOND-DU-LAC

On Fond-du-lac's shore I'm hearin' once more that blessed
old grammyfone play.

The summer's all gone, an' I'm still livin' on in the same
old haphazardous way.

Oh, I cut out the booze, an' with muscles an' thews I
corralled all the coin to go back;

But it wasn't to be: he'd a mother, you see, so I —
*slipped it to Four-finger Jack.*

## THE LAND OF BEYOND

HAVE ever you heard of the Land of Beyond,
       That dreams at the gates of the day?
Alluring it lies at the skirts of the skies,
       And ever so far away;
Alluring it calls: O ye the yoke galls,
       And ye of the trail overfond,
With saddle and pack, by paddle and track,
       Let's go to the Land of Beyond!

Have ever you stood where the silences brood,
       And vast the horizons begin,
At the dawn of the day to behold far away
       The goal you would strive for and win?
Yet ah! in the night when you gain to the height,
       With the vast pool of heaven star-spawned,
Afar and agleam, like a valley of dream,
       Still mocks you a Land of Beyond.

# THE LAND OF BEYOND

Thank God! there is always a Land of Beyond
    For us who are true to the trail;
A vision to seek, a beckoning peak,
    A farness that never will fail;
A pride in our soul that mocks at a goal,
    A manhood that irks at a bond,
And try how we will, unattainable still,
    Behold it, our Land of Beyond!

## SUNSHINE

### I

FLAT as a drum-head stretch the haggard snows;
The mighty skies are palisades of light;
The stars are blurred; the silence grows and grows;
Vaster and vaster vaults the icy night.
Here in my sleeping-bag I cower and pray:
"Silence and night, have pity! stoop and slay."

I have not slept for many, many days.
I close my eyes with weariness — that's all.
I still have strength to feed the drift-wood blaze,
That flickers weirdly on the icy wall.
I still have strength to pray: "God rest her soul,
Here in the awful shadow of the Pole."

There in the cabin's alcove low she lies,
Still candles gleaming at her head and feet;
All snow-drop white, ash-cold, with coséd eyes,
Lips smiling, hands at rest — O God, how sweet!
How all unutterably sweet she seems. . . .
Not dead, not dead indeed — she dreams, she dreams.

## II

"Sunshine," I called her, and she brought, I vow,
  God's blessed sunshine to this life of mine.
I was a rover, of the breed who plough
Life's furrow in a far-flung, lonely line;
The wilderness my home, my fortune cast
In a wild land of dearth, barbaric, vast.

When did I see her first?  Long had I lain
Groping my way to life through fevered gloom.
Sudden the cloud of darkness left my brain;
A velvet bar of sunshine pierced the room,
And in that mellow glory aureoled
She stood, she stood, all golden in its gold.

Sunshine!  O miracle! the earth grew glad;
Radiant each blade of grass, each living thing.
What a huge strength, high hope, proud will I had!
All the wide world with rapture seemed to ring.
Would she but wed me?   *Yes:* then fared we forth
Into the vast, unvintageable North.

# SUNSHINE

## III

*In Muskrat Land the conies leap,*
*The wavies linger in their flight;*
*The jewelled, snakelike rivers creep;*
*The sun, sad rogue, is out all night;*
*The great wood bison paws the sand,*
*In Muskrat Land, in Muskrat Land.*

*In Muskrat Land dim streams divide*
*The tundras belted by the sky.*
*How sweet in slim canoe to glide,*
*And dream, and let the world go by!*
*Build gay camp-fires on greening strand!*
*In Muskrat Land, in Muskrat Land.*

## SUNSHINE

### IV

And so we dreamed and drifted, she and I;
And how she loved that free, unfathomed life!
There in the peach-bloom of the midnight sky,
The silence welded us, true man and wife.
Then North and North invincibly we pressed
Beyond the Circle, to the world's white crest.

And on the wind-flailed Arctic waste we stayed,
Dwelt with the Huskies by the Polar sea.
Fur had they, white fox, marten, mink to trade,
And we had food-stuff, bacon, flour and tea.
So we made snug, chummed up with all the band:
Sudden the Winter swooped on Husky Land.

## V

What was that ill so sinister and dread,
Smiting the tribe with sickness to the bone?
So that we waked one morn to find them fled;
So that we stood and stared, alone, alone.
Bravely she smiled and looked into my eyes;
Laughed at their troubled, stern, foreboding pain;
Gaily she mocked the menace of the skies,
Turned to our cheery cabin once again,
Saying: " 'Twill soon be over, dearest one,
The long, long night: then O the sun, the sun!"

# SUNSHINE

## VI

God made a heart of gold, of gold,
Shining and sweet and true;
Gave it a home of fairest mould,
Blest it, and called it — You.

God gave the rose its grace of glow,
And the lark its radiant glee;
But, better than all, I know, I know
God gave you, Heart, to me.

## VII

She was all sunshine in those dubious days;
Our cabin beaconed with defiant light;
We chattered by the friendly drift-wood blaze;
Closer and closer cowered the hag-like night.
A wolf-howl would have been a welcome sound,
And there was none in all that stricken land;
Yet with such silence, darkness, death around,
Learned we to love as few can understand.
Spirit with spirit fused, and soul with soul,
There in the sullen shadow of the Pole.

## VIII

What was that haunting horror of the night?
Brave was she; buoyant, full of sunny cheer.
Why was her face so small, so strangely white?
Then did I turn from her, heart-sick with fear;
Sought in my agony the outcast snows;
Prayed in my pain to that insensate sky;
Grovelled and sobbed and cursed, and then arose:
"Sunshine! O heart of gold! to die! to die!"

## IX

She died on Christmas day — it seems so sad
That one you love should die on Christmas day.
Head-bowed I knelt by her; O God! I had
No tears to shed, no moan, no prayer to pray.
I heard her whisper: "Call me, will you, dear?
They say Death parts, but I won't go away.
I will be with you in the cabin here;
Oh I will plead with God to let me stay!
Stay till the Night is gone, till Spring is nigh,
Till sunshine comes . . . be brave . . . I'm
    tired . . . good-bye. . . ."

# SUNSHINE

## X

For weeks, for months I have not seen the sun;
The minatory dawns are leprous pale;
The felon days malinger one by one;
How like a dream Life is! how vain! how stale!
I, too, am faint; that vampire-like disease
Has fallen on me; weak and cold am I,
Hugging a tiny fire in fear I freeze:
The cabin must be cold, and so I try
To bear the frost, the frost that fights decay,
The frost that keeps her beautiful alway.

# SUNSHINE

## XI

She lies within an icy vault;
It glitters like a cave of salt.
All marble-pure and angel-sweet
With candles at her head and feet,
Under an ermine robe she lies.
I kiss her hands, I kiss her eyes:
" Come back, come back, O Love, I pray,
Into this house, this house of clay!
Answer my kisses soft and warm;
Nestle again within my arm.
Come! for I know that you are near;
Open your eyes and look, my dear.
Just for a moment break the mesh;
Back from the spirit leap to flesh.
Weary I wait; the night is black;
Love of my life, come back, come back! "

## XII

Last night maybe I was a little mad,
For as I prayed despairful by her side,
Such a strange, antic visioning I had:
Lo! it did seem *her eyes were open wide.*
Surely I must have dreamed! I stared once
    more.  .  .  .
No, 'twas a candle's trick, a shadow cast.
There were her lashes locking as before.
(Oh, but it filled me with a joy so vast!)
No, 'twas a freak, a fancy of the brain,
(Oh, but to-night I'll try again, again!)

## SUNSHINE

### XIII

It was no dream; now do I know that Love
Leapt from the starry battlements of Death;
For in my vigil as I bent above,
Calling her name with eager, burning breath,
Sudden there came a change: again I saw
The radiance of the rose-leaf stain her cheek;
Rivers of rapture thrilled in sunny thaw;
Cleft were her coral lips as if to speak;
Curved were her tender arms as if to cling;
Open the flower-like eyes of lucent blue,
Looking at me with love so pitying
That I could fancy Heaven shining through.
"Sunshine," I faltered, "stay with me, oh, stay!"
Yet ere I finished, in a moment's flight,
There in her angel purity she lay —
Ah! but I know she'll come again to-night.
*Even as radiant sword leaps from the sheath,*
*Soul from the body leaps — we call it Death.*

## XIV

Even as this line I write,
Do I know that she is near;
Happy am I, every night
Comes she back to bid me cheer;
Kissing her, I hold her fast;
Win her into life at last.

Did I dream that yesterday
On yon mountain ridge a glow
Soft as moonstone paled away,
Leaving less forlorn the snow?
Could it be the sun?  Oh, fain
Would I see the sun again!

Oh, to see a coral dawn
Gladden to a crocus glow!
Day's a spectre dim and wan,
Dancing on the furtive snow;
Night's a cloud upon my brain:
Oh, to see the sun again!

You who find us in this place,
Have you pity in your breast;
Let us in our last embrace,
Under earth sun-hallowed rest.
Night's a claw upon my brain:
Oh, to see the sun again!

## SUNSHINE

### XV

The Sun! at last the Sun! I write these lines,
Here on my knees, with feeble, fumbling hand.
Look! in yon mountain cleft a radiance shines,
Gleam of a primrose — see it thrill, expand,
Grow glorious. Dear God be praised! it streams
Into the cabin in a gush of gold.
Look! there she stands, the angel of my dreams,
All in the radiant shimmer aureoled;
First as I saw her from my bed of pain;
First as I loved her when the darkness passed.
Now do I know that Life is not in vain;
Now do I know God cares, at last, at last!
Light outlives dark, joy grief, and Love's the sum:
Heart of my heart! Sunshine! I come . . . I
    come. . . .

## THE IDEALIST

OH you who have daring deeds to tell!
  And you who have felt Ambition's spell!
Have you heard of the louse who longed to dwell
  In the golden hair of a queen?
He sighed all day and he sighed all night,
  And no one could understand it quite,
For the head of a slut is a louse's delight,
  But he pined for the head of a queen.

So he left his kinsfolk in merry play,
  And off by his lonesome he stole away,
From the home of his youth so bright and gay,
  And gloriously unclean.
And at last he came to the palace gate,
  And he made his way in a manner straight
(For a louse may go where a man must wait)
  To the tiring-room of the queen.

## THE IDEALIST

The queen she spake to her tiring-maid:
"There's something the matter, I'm afraid.
To-night ere for sleep my hair ye braid,
    Just see what may be seen."
And lo, when they combed that shining hair
    They found him alone in his glory there,
And he cried: "I die, but I do not care,
    For I've lived in the head of a queen!"

WHEN the boys come out from Lac Labiche in the
   lure of the early Spring,
To take the pay of the " Hudson's Bay," as their fathers
   did before,
They are all a-glee for the jamboree, and they make the
   Landing ring
With a whoop and a whirl, and a " Grab your girl," and
   a rip and a skip and a roar.
For the spree of Spring is a sacred thing, and the boys
   must have their fun;
Packer and tracker and half-breed Cree, from the boat
   to the bar they leap;
And then when the long flotilla goes, and the last of
   their pay is done,
The boys from the banks of Lac Labiche swing to the
   heavy sweep.
And oh, how they sigh! and their throats are dry, and
   sorry are they and sick:
Yet there's none so cursed with a lime-kiln thirst as that
   Athabaska Dick.

He was long and slim and lean of limb, but strong as a
    stripling bear;
And by the right of his skill and might he guided the
    Long Brigade.
All water-wise were his laughing eyes, and he steered
    with a careless care,
And he shunned the shock of foam and rock, till they
    came to the Big Cascade.
And here they must make the long *portāge,* and the
    boys sweat in the sun;
And they heft and pack, and they haul and track, and
    each must do his trick;
But their thoughts are far in the Landing bar, where
    the founts of nectar run:
And no man thinks of such gorgeous drinks as that
    Athabaska Dick.

'Twas the close of day and his long boat lay just over
    the Big Cascade,
When there came to him one Jack-pot Jim, with a wild
    light in his eye;
And he softly laughed, and he led Dick aft, all eager,
    yet half afraid,
And snugly stowed in his coat he showed a pilfered
    flask of " rye."

And in haste he slipped, or in fear he tripped, but —
  Dick in warning roared —
And there rang a yell, and it befell that Jim was over-
  board.

Oh, I heard a splash, and quick as a flash I knew he
  could not swim.
I saw him whirl in the river swirl, and thresh his arms
  about.
In a queer, strained way I heard Dick say: " I'm going
  after him,"
Throw off his coat, leap down the boat — and then I
  gave a shout:
" Boys, grab him, quick!  You're crazy, Dick!  Far better one than two!
" Hell, man!  You know you've got no show!  It's sure
  and certain death. . . ."
And there we hung, and there we clung, with beef and
  brawn and thew,
And sinews cracked and joints were racked, and panting
  came our breath;
And there we swayed and there we prayed, till strength
  and hope were spent —
Then Dick, he threw us off like rats, and after Jim he
  went.

With mighty urge amid the surge of river-rage he leapt,
And gripped his mate and desperate he fought to gain
the shore;
With teeth a-gleam he bucked the stream, yet swift and
sure he swept
To meet the mighty cataract that waited all a-roar.
And there we stood like carven wood, our faces sickly
white,
And watched him as he beat the foam, and inch by inch
he lost;
And nearer, nearer drew the fall, and fiercer grew the
fight,
Till on the very cascade crest a last farewell he tossed.
Then down and down and down they plunged into that
pit of dread;
And mad we tore along the shore to claim our bitter
dead.


And from that hell of frenzied foam, that crashed and
fumed and boiled,
Two little bodies bubbled up, and they were heedless
then;
And oh, they lay like senseless clay! and bitter hard we
toiled,

Yet never, never gleam of hope, and we were weary men.

And moments mounted into hours, and black was our
despair;

And faint were we, and we were fain to give them up
as dead,

When suddenly I thrilled with hope: " Back, boys! and
give him air;

" I feel the flutter of his heart. . . ." And, as the
word I said,

Dick gave a sigh, and gazed around, and saw our breath-
less band;

And saw the sky's blue floor above, all strewn with
golden fleece;

And saw his comrade Jack-pot Jim, and touched him
with his hand:

And then there came into his eyes a look of perfect
peace.

And as there, at his very feet, the thwarted river raved,

I heard him murmur low and deep:

" Thank God! the *whiskey's* saved."

## CHEER

IT'S a mighty good world, so it is, dear lass,
    When even the worst is said.
There's a smile and a tear, a sigh and a cheer,
    But better be living than dead;
A joy and a pain, a loss and a gain;
    There's honey and may be some gall:
Yet still I declare, foul weather or fair,
    It's a mighty good world after all.

For look, lass! at night when I break from the fight,
    My Kingdom's awaiting for me;
There's comfort and rest, and the warmth of your breast,
    And little ones climbing my knee.
There's fire-light and song — Oh, the world may be
        wrong!
    Its empires may topple and fall:
My home is my care — if gladness be there,
    It's a mighty good world after all.

## CHEER

O heart of pure gold! I have made you a fold,
    It's sheltered, sun-fondled and warm.
O little ones, rest! I have fashioned a nest;
    Sleep on! you are safe from the storm.
For there's no foe like fear, and there's no friend like
        cheer,
    And sunshine will flash at our call;
So crown Love as King, and let us all sing —
    "It's a mighty good world after all."

## THE RETURN

THEY turned him loose; he bowed his head,
    A felon, bent and grey.
His face was even as the Dead,
    He had no word to say.

He sought the home of his old love,
    To look on her once more;
And where her roses breathed above,
    He cowered beside the door.

She sat there in the shining room;
    Her hair was silver grey.
He stared and stared from out the gloom;
    He turned to go away.

Her roses rustled overhead.
    She saw, with sudden start.
"I knew that you would come," she said,
    And held him to her heart.

## THE RETURN

Her face was rapt and angel-sweet;
   She touched his hair of grey;

.    .    .    .    .    .    .

*But he, sob-shaken, at her feet,
   Could only pray and pray.*

## THE JUNIOR GOD

THE Junior God looked from his place
  In the conning towers of heaven,
And he saw the world through the span of space
  Like a giant golf-ball driven.
And because he was bored, as some gods are,
  With high celestial mirth,
He clutched the reins of a shooting star,
  And he steered it down to earth.

The Junior God, 'mid leaf and bud,
  Passed on with a weary air,
Till lo! he came to a pool of mud,
  And some hogs were rolling there.
Then in he plunged with gleeful cries,
  And down he lay supine;
For they had no mud in paradise,
  And they likewise had no swine.

The Junior God forgot himself;
  He squelched mud through his toes;
With the careless joy of a wanton boy
  His reckless laughter rose.

Till, tired at last, in a brook close by,
    He washed off every stain;
Then softly up to the radiant sky
    He rose, a god again.

The Junior God now heads the roll
    In the list of heaven's peers;
He sits in the House of High Control,
    And he regulates the spheres.
Yet does he wonder, do you suppose,
    If, even in gods divine,
The best and wisest may not be those
    Who have wallowed awhile with the swine?

## THE NOSTOMANIAC

*O*N *the ragged edge of the world I'll roam,*
  *And the home of the wolf shall be my home,*
*And a bunch of bones on the boundless snows*
*The end of my trail . . . who knows, who knows!*


I'm dreaming to-night in the fire-glow, alone in my study
  tower,
My books battalioned around me, my Kipling flat on my
  knee;
But I'm not in the mood for reading, I haven't moved
  for an hour;
Body and brain I'm weary, weary the heart of me;
Weary of crushing a longing it's little I understand,
For I thought that my trail was ended, I thought I had
  earned my rest;
But oh, it's stronger than life is, the call of the hearthless
  land!
And I turn to the North in my trouble, as a child to the
  mother-breast.

Here in my den it's quiet; the sea-wind taps on the pane;
There's comfort and ease and plenty, the smile of the
    South is sweet.
All that a man might long for, fight for and seek in vain,
Pictures and books and music, pleasure my last retreat.
Peace! I thought I had gained it, I swore that my tale
    was told;
By my hair that is grey I swore it, by my eyes that are
    slow to see;
Yet what does it all avail me? to-night, to-night as of old,
Out of the dark I hear it — the Northland calling to me.


And I'm daring a rampageous river that runs the devil
    knows where;
My hand is athrill on the paddle, the birch-bark bounds
    like a bird.
Hark to the rumble of rapids! Here in my morris chair
Eager and tense I'm straining — isn't it most absurd?
Now in the churn and the lather, foam that hisses and
    stings,
Leap I, keyed for the struggle, fury and fume and roar;
Rocks are spitting like hell-cats — Oh, it's a sport for
    kings,
Life on a twist of the paddle . . . there's my
    " Kim " on the floor.

How I thrill and I vision! Then my camp of a night;
Red and gold of the fire-glow, net afloat in the stream;
Scent of the pines and silence, little " pal " pipe alight,
Body a-purr with pleasure, sleep untroubled of dream:
Banquet of paystreak bacon! moment of joy divine,
When the bannock is hot and gluey, and the teapot's
    nearing the boil!
Never was wolf so hungry, stomach cleaving to
    spine. . . .
Ha! there's my servant calling, says that dinner will
    spoil.

What do I want with dinner? Can I eat any more?
Can I sleep as I used to? . . . Oh, I abhor this
    life!
Give me the Great Uncertain, the Barren Land for a
    floor,
The Milky Way for a roof-beam, splendour and space
    and strife:
Something to fight and die for — the limpid Lake of
    the Bear,
The Empire of Empty Bellies, the dunes where the Dog-
    ribs dwell;
Big things, real things, live things . . . here on
    my morris chair
How I ache for the Northland! " Dinner and serv-
    ants "— Hell!!

Am I too old, I wonder?  Can I take one trip more?
Go to the granite-ribbed valleys, flooded with sunset
　　wine,
Peaks that pierce the aurora, rivers I must explore,
Lakes of a thousand islands, millioning hordes of the
　　Pine?
Do they not miss me, I wonder, valley and peak and
　　plain?
Whispering each to the other: " Many a moon has
　　passed . . .
" Where has he gone, our lover?  Will he come back
　　again?
" Star with his fires our tundra, leave us his bones at
　　last? "


Yes, I'll go back to the Northland, back to the way of
　　the bear,
Back to the muskeg and mountain, back to the ice-
　　leaguered sea.
Old am I!  what does it matter?  Nothing I would
　　not dare;
Give me a trail to conquer — Oh, it is " meat " to me!
I will go back to the Northland, feeble and blind and
　　lame;

Sup with the sunny-eyed Husky, eat moose-nose with the
    Cree;
Play with the Yellow-knife bastards, boasting my blood
    and my name:
I will go back to the Northland, for the Northland is
    calling to me.


Then give to me paddle and whiplash, and give to me
    tumpline and gun;
Give to me salt and tobacco, flour and a gunny of tea;
Take me up over the Circle, under the flamboyant sun;
Turn me foot-loose like a savage — that is the finish
    of me.
I know the trail I am seeking, it's up by the Lake of the
    Bear;
It's down by the Arctic Barrens, it's over to Hudson's
    Bay;
Maybe I'll get there,— maybe: death is set by a
    hair. . . .
Hark! it's the Northland calling! now must I go
    away. . . .


    *Go to the Wild that waits for me;*
    *Go where the moose and the musk-ox be;*
    *Go to the wolf and the secret snows;*
    *Go to my fate . . . who knows, who knows!*

## *AMBITION*

**T**HEY brought the mighty chief to town;
 They showed him strange, unwonted sights;
Yet as he wandered up and down,
He seemed to scorn their vain delights.
His face was grim, his eye lacked fire,
As one who mourns a glory dead;
And when they sought his heart's desire:
"Me like'um tooth same gold," he said.

A dental place they quickly found.
He neither moaned nor moved his head.
They pulled his teeth so white and sound;
They put in teeth of gold instead.
Oh, never saw I man so gay!
His very being seemed to swell:
"Ha! ha!" he cried, "Now Injun say
Me heap big chief, *me look like hell.*"

## TO SUNNYDALE

THERE lies the trail to Sunnydale,
  Amid the lure of laughter.
Oh, how can we unhappy be
Beneath its leafy rafter!
Each perfect hour is like a flower,
Each day is like a posy.
How can you say the skies are grey?
You're wrong, my friend, they're rosy.

With right good will let's climb the hill,
And leave behind all sorrow.
Oh, we'll be gay! a bright to-day
Will make a bright to-morrow.
Oh, we'll be strong! the way is long
That never has a turning;
The hill is high, but there's the sky,
And how the West is burning!

And if through chance of circumstance
We have to go bare-foot, sir,
We'll not repine — a friend of mine
Has got no feet to boot, sir.
This Happiness a habit is,
And Life is what we make it:
See! there's the trail to Sunnydale!
Up, friend! and let us take it.

## THE BLIND AND THE DEAD

SHE lay like a saint on her copper couch;
    Like an angel asleep she lay,
In the stare of the ghoulish folks that slouch
    Past the Dead and sneak away.

Then came old Jules of the sightless gaze,
    Who begged in the streets for bread.
Each day he had come for a year of days,
    And groped his way to the Dead.

"What's the Devil's Harvest to-day?" he cried;
    "A wanton with eyes of blue!
I've known too many a such," he sighed;
    "Maybe I know this . . . mon Dieu!"

He raised the head of the heedless Dead;
    He fingered the frozen face. . . .
Then a deathly spell on the watchers fell —
    God! it was still, that place!

He raised the head of the careless Dead;
    He fumbled a vagrant curl;
And then with his sightless smile he said:
    "It's only my little girl."

"Dear, my dear, did they hurt you so!
    Come to your daddy's heart. . . ."
Aye, and he held so tight, you know,
    They were hard to force apart.

No! Paris isn't always gay;
    And the morgue has its stories too:
You are a writer of tales, you say —
    Then there is a tale for you.

## THE ATAVIST

WHAT are you doing here, Tom Thorne, on the
   white top-knot o' the world,
Where the wind has the cut of a naked knife and the
   stars are rapier keen?
Hugging a smudgy willow fire, deep in a lynx robe curled,
You that's a lord's own son, Tom Thorne — what does
   your madness mean?

Go home, go home to your clubs, Tom Thorne! home to
   your evening dress!
Home to your place of power and pride, and the feast
   that waits for you!
Why do you linger all alone in the splendid emptiness,
Scouring the Land of the Little Sticks on the trail of
   the caribou?

Why did you fall off the Earth, Tom Thorne, out of
   our social ken?
What did your deep damnation prove? What was your
   dark despair?

Oh with the width of a world between, and years to the
    count of ten,
If they cut out your heart to-night, Tom Thorne, *Her*
    name would be graven there!


And you fled afar for the thing called Peace, and you
    thought you would find it here,
In the purple tundras vastly spread, and the mountains
    whitely piled;
It's a weary quest and a dreary quest, but I think that
    the end is near;
For they say that the Lord has hidden it in the secret
    heart of the Wild.


And you know that heart as few men know, and your
    eyes are fey and deep,
With a " something lost " come welling back from the
    raw, red dawn of life:
With woe and pain have you greatly lain, till out of
    abysmal sleep
The soul of the Stone Age leaps in you, alert for the
    ancient strife.

And if you came to our feast again, with its pomp and
    glee and glow,
I think you would sit stone-still, Tom Thorne, and see
    in a daze of dream,
A mad sun goading to frenzied flame the glittering gems
    of the snow,
And a monster musk-ox bulking black against the blood-
    red gleam.

I think you would see berg-battling shores, and stammer
    and halt and stare,
With a sudden sense of the frozen void, serene and
    vast and still;
And the aching gleam and the hush of dream, and the
    track of a great white bear,
And the primal lust that surged in you as you sprang
    to make your kill.

I think you would hear the bull-moose call, and the
    glutted river roar;
And spy the hosts of the caribou shadow the shining
    plain;
And feel the pulse of the Silences, and stand elate once
    more
On the verge of the yawning vastitudes that call to you
    in vain.

For I think you are one with the stars and the sun, and
the wind and the wave and the dew;
And the peaks untrod that yearn to God, and the valleys
undefiled;
Men soar with wings, and they bridle kings, but what
is it all to you,
Wise in the ways of the wilderness, and strong with the
strength of the Wild?

You have spent your life, you have waged your strife
where never we play a part;
You have held the throne of the Great Unknown, you
have ruled a kingdom vast:

. . . . . . .

*But to-night there's a strange, new trail for you, and you
go, O weary heart!*
*To the peace and rest of the Great Unguessed . .
at last, Tom Thorne, at last.*

## THE SCEPTIC

MY Father Christmas passed away
    When I was barely seven.
At twenty-one, alack-a-day,
I lost my hope of heaven.

Yet not in either lies the curse:
The hell of it's because
I don't know which loss hurt the worse —
My God or Santa Claus.

## THE ROVER

### I

OH, how good it is to be
    Foot-loose and heart-free!
Just my dog and pipe and I, underneath the vast sky;
Trail to try and goal to win, white road and cool inn;
Fields to lure a lad afar, clear spring and still star;
Lilting feet that never tire, green dingle, fagot fire;
None to hurry, none to hold, heather hill and hushed fold;
Nature like a picture book, laughing leaf and bright
    brook;
Every day a jewel bright, set serenely in the night;
Every night a holy shrine, radiant for a day divine.

Weathered cheek and kindly eye, let the wanderer go by.
Woman-love and wistful heart, let the gipsy one depart.
For the farness and the road are his glory and his goad.
Oh, the lilt of youth and Spring! Eyes laugh and lips
    sing.

            Yea, but it is good to be
            Foot-loose and heart-free!

## THE ROVER

### II

Yet how good it is to come
Home at last, home, home!
On the clover swings the bee, overhead's the hale tree
Sky of turquoise gleams through, yonder glints the lake's
blue.
In a hammock let's swing, weary of wandering;
Tired of wild, uncertain lands, strange faces, faint hands

Has the wondrous world gone cold? Am I growing
old, old?
Grey and weary . . . let me dream, glide on the
tranquil stream.
Oh, what joyous days I've had, full, fervid, gay, glad!
Yet there comes a subtile change, let the stripling rove,
range.
From sweet roving comes sweet rest, after all, home's
best.
And if there's a little bit of woman-love with it,
I will count my life content, God-blest and well
spent. . . .

Oh but it is good to be
Foot-loose and heart-free!
Yet how good it is to come
Home at last, home, home!

A T dawn of day the white land lay all gruesome-
like and grim,

When Bill Mc'Gee he says to me: "We've *got* to do it,
Jim.

"We've got to make Fort Liard quick. I know the
river's bad,

"But, oh! the little woman's sick . . . why! don't
you savvy, lad?"

And me! Well, yes, I must confess it wasn't hard to
see

Their little family group of two would soon be one of
three.

And so I answered, careless-like: "Why, Bill! you don't
suppose

"I'm scared of that there 'babbling brook'? Whatever
you say — goes."


A real live man was Barb-wire Bill, with insides copper-
lined;

For "barb-wire" was the brand of "hooch" to which
he most inclined.

They knew him far; his igloos are on Kittiegazuit strand.

62

They knew him well, the tribes who dwell within the
    Barren Land.
From Koyokuk to Kuskoquim his fame was everywhere;
And he did love, all life above, that little Julie Claire,
The lithe, white slave-girl he had bought for seven hun-
    dred skins,
And taken to his wickiup to make his moccasins.


We crawled down to the river bank and feeble folk
    were we,
That Julie Claire from God-knows-where, and Barb-wire
    Bill and me.
From shore to shore we heard the roar the heaving ice-
    floes make,
And loud we laughed, and launched our raft, and fol-
    lowed in their wake.
The river swept and seethed and leapt, and caught us
    in its stride;
And on we hurled amid a world that crashed on every
    side.
With sullen din the banks caved in; the shore-ice lanced
    the stream;
The naked floes like spooks arose, all jiggling and agleam.
Black anchor-ice of strange device shot upward from its
    bed,
As night and day we cleft our way, and arrow-like we
    sped.

But " Faster still! " cried Barb-wire Bill, and looked the
    live-long day
In dull despair at Julie Claire, as white like death she
    lay.
And sometimes he would seem to pray and sometimes
    seem to curse,
And bent above, with eyes of love, yet ever she grew
    worse.
And as we plunged and leapt and lunged, her face was
    plucked with pain,
And I could feel his nerves of steel a-quiver at the strain.
And in the night he gripped me tight as I lay fast asleep:
" The river's kicking like a steer . . . run out the
    forward sweep!
" That's Hell-gate Canyon right ahead; I know of old
    its roar,
" And . . . I'll be damned! *the ice is jammed!*
    We've *got* to make the shore."


With one wild leap I gripped the sweep.  The night was
    black as sin.
The float-ice crashed and ripped and smashed, and stunned
    us with its din.
And near and near, and clear and clear I heard the can-
    yon boom;

And swift and strong we swept along to meet our awful
    doom.
And as with dread I glimpsed ahead the death that waited
    there,
My only thought was of the girl, the little Julie Claire;
And so, like demon mad with fear, I panted at the oar,
And foot by foot, and inch by inch, we worked the raft
    ashore.


The bank was staked with grinding ice, and as we scraped
    and crashed,
I only knew one thing to do, and through my mind it
    flashed:
Yet while I groped to find the rope, I heard Bill's savage
    cry:
"That's my job, lad! It's me that jumps. I'll snub
    this raft or die!"
I saw him leap, I saw him creep, I saw him gain the
    land;
I saw him crawl, I saw him fall, then run with rope in
    hand.
And then the darkness gulped him up, and down we
    dashed once more,
And nearer, nearer drew the jam, and thunder-like its
    roar.

Oh God! all's lost . . . from Julie Claire there
    came a wail of pain,
And then — the rope grew sudden taut, and quivered at
    the strain;
It slacked and slipped, it whined and gripped, and oh, I
    held my breath!
And there we hung and there we swung right in the
    jaws of death.

A little strand of hempen rope, and how I watched it
    there,
With all around a hell of sound, and darkness and despair;
A little strand of hempen rope, I watched it all alone,
And somewhere in the dark behind I heard a woman
    moan;
And somewhere in the dark ahead I heard a man cry out,
Then silence, silence, silence fell, and mocked my hollow
    shout.
And yet once more from out the shore I heard that cry
    of pain,
A moan of mortal agony, then all was still again.

That night was hell with all the frills, and when the
    dawn broke dim,
I saw a lean and level land, but never sign of him.
I saw a flat and frozen shore of hideous device,

I saw a long-drawn strand of rope that vanished through the ice.

And on that treeless, rockless shore I found my partner — dead.

No place was there to snub the raft, so — *he had served instead;*

And with the rope lashed round his waist, in last defiant fight,

He'd thrown himself beneath the ice, that closed and gripped him tight;

And there he'd held us back from death, as fast in death he lay. . . .

Say, boys! I'm not the pious brand, but — I just tried to pray.

And then I looked to Julie Claire, and sore abashed was I,

For from the robes that covered her, *I — heard — a — baby — cry.* . . .

Thus was Love conqueror of death, and life for life was given;

And though no saint on earth, d'ye think — Bill's squared hisself with Heaven?

## "?"

IF you had the choice of two women to wed,
  (Though of course the idea is quite absurd)
And the first from her heels to her dainty head
Was charming in every sense of the word:
And yet in the past (I grieve to state),
She never had been exactly " straight."

And the second — she was beyond all cavil,
A model of virtue, I must confess;
And yet, alas! she was dull as the devil,
And rather a dowd in the way of dress;
Though what she was lacking in wit and beauty,
She more than made up for in " sense of duty."

Now, suppose you must wed, and make no blunder,
And either would love you, and let you win her —
Which of the two would you choose, I wonder,
The stolid saint or the sparkling sinner?

## JUST THINK!

JUST think! some night the stars will gleam
    Upon a cold, grey stone,
And trace a name with silver beam,
    And lo! 'twill be your own.

That night is speeding on to greet
    Your epitaphic rhyme.
Your life is but a little beat
    Within the heart of Time.

A little gain, a little pain,
    A laugh, lest you may moan;
A little blame, a little fame,
    A star-gleam on a stone.

## THE LUNGER

JACK would laugh an' joke all day;
     Never saw a lad so gay;
Singin' like a medder lark,
Loaded to the Plimsoll mark
With God's sunshine was that boy;
Had a strangle-holt on Joy.
Held his head 'way up in air,
Left no callin' cards on Care;
Breezy, buoyant, brave and true;
Sent his sunshine out to you;
Cheerfulest when clouds was black —
     Happy Jack!  Oh, Happy Jack!

Sittin' in my shack alone
I could hear him in his own,
Singin' far into the night,
Till it didn't seem just right
One man should corral the fun,
Live his life so in the sun;
Didn't seem quite natural
Not to have a grouch at all;
Not a trouble, not a lack —
     Happy Jack!  Oh, Happy Jack!

# THE LUNGER

He was plumbful of good cheer
Till he struck that low-down year;
Got so thin, so little to him,
You could most see day-light through him.
Never was his eye so bright,
Never was his cheek so white.
Seemed as if somethin' was wrong,
Sort o' quaver in his song.
Same old smile, same hearty voice:
"Bless you, boys! let's all rejoice!"
But old Doctor shook his head:
"Half a lung," was all he said.
Yet that half was surely right,
For I heard him every night,
Singin', singin' in his shack —
     Happy Jack! Oh, Happy Jack!

Then one day a letter came
Endin' with a female name;
Seemed to get him in the neck,
Sort o' pile-driver effect;
Paled his lip and plucked his breath,
Left him starin' still as death.
Somethin' had gone awful wrong,
Yet that night he sang his song.
Oh, but it was good to hear!

For there clutched my heart a fear,
So that I quaked listenin'
Every night to hear him sing.
But each day he laughed with me,
An' his smile was full of glee.
Nothin' seemed to set him back —
    Happy Jack! Oh, Happy Jack!

Then one night the singin' stopped . . .
Seemed as if my heart just flopped;
For I'd learned to love the boy
With his gilt-edged line of joy,
With his glorious gift of bluff,
With his splendid fightin' stuff.
Sing on, lad, and play the game!
O dear God! . . . no singin' came.
But there surged to me instead —
Silence, silence, deep and dread;
Till I shuddered, tried to pray,
Said: " He's maybe gone away."

Oh, yes, he had gone away,
Gone forever and a day.
But he'd left behind him there,
In his cabin, pinched and bare,
His poor body, skin and bone,

## THE LUNGER

His sharp face, cold as a stone.
An' his stiffened fingers pressed
Somethin' bright upon his breast:
Locket with a silken curl,
Poor, sweet portrait of a girl.
Yet I reckon at the last
How defiant-like he passed;
For there sat upon his lips
Smile that death could not eclipse;
An' within his eyes lived still
Joy that dyin' could not kill.

An' now when the nights are long,
How I miss his cheery song!
How I sigh an' wish him back!
    Happy Jack! Oh, Happy Jack!

## THE MOUNTAIN AND THE LAKE

I KNOW a mountain thrilling to the stars,
   Peerless and pure, and pinnacled with snow;
Glimpsing the golden dawn o'er coral bars,
Flaunting the vanisht sunset's garnet glow;
Proudly patrician, passionless, serene;
Soaring in silvered steeps where cloud-surfs break;
Virgin and vestal — Oh, a very Queen!
And at her feet there dreams a quiet lake.

My lake adores my mountain — well I know,
For I have watched it from its dawn-dream start,
Stilling its mirror to her splendid snow,
Framing her image in its trembling heart;
Glassing her graciousness of greening wood,
Kissing her throne, melodiously mad,
Thrilling responsive to her every mood,
Gloomed with her sadness, gay when she is glad.

## THE MOUNTAIN AND THE LAKE

My lake has dreamed and loved since time was born;
Will love and dream till time shall cease to be;
Gazing to Her in worship half forlorn,
Who looks towards the stars and will not see —
My peerless mountain, splendid in her scorn. . . .
Alas! poor little lake! Alas! poor me!

M OKO, the Educated Ape is here,
      The pet of vaudeville, so the posters say,
  And every night the gaping people pay
To see him in his panoply appear;
To see him pad his paunch with dainty cheer,
  Puff his perfecto, swill champagne, and sway
  Just like a gentleman, yet all in play,
Then bow himself off stage with brutish leer.

And as to-night, with noble knowledge crammed,
  I 'mid this human compost take my place,
I, once a poet, now so dead and damned,
  The woeful tears half freezing on my face:
" O God! " I cry, " let me but take his shape,
  Moko's, the Blest, the Educated Ape."

## DEATH IN THE ARCTIC

### I

I TOOK the clock down from the shelf;
  " At eight," said I, " I shoot myself."
It lacked a *minute* of the hour,
And as I waited all a-cower,
A skinful of black, boding pain,
Bits of my life came back again.  .  .  .

*" Mother, there's nothing more to eat —*
  *Why don't you go out on the street?*
*Always you sit and cry and cry;*
*Here at my play I wonder why.*
*Mother, when you dress up at night,*
*Red are your cheeks, your eyes are bright;*
*Twining a ribband in your hair,*
*Kissing good-bye you go down-stair.*
*Then I'm as lonely as can be.*
*Oh, how I wish you were with me!*
*Yet when you go out on the street,*
*Mother, there's always lots to eat.  .  .*

## II

For days the igloo has been dark;
But now the rag wick sends a spark
That glitters in the icy air,
And wakes frost sapphires everywhere;
Bright, bitter flames, that adder-like
Dart here and there, yet fear to strike
The gruesome gloom wherein *they* lie,
My comrades, oh, so keen to die!
And I, the last — well, here I wait
The clock to strike the hour of eight. . . .

" *Boy, it is bitter to be hurled*
*Nameless and naked on the world;*
*Frozen by night and starved by day,*
*Curses and kicks and clouts your pay.*
*But you must fight!   Boy, look on me!*
*Anarch of all earth-misery;*
*Beggar and tramp and shameless sot;*
*Emblem of ill, in rags that rot.*
*Would you be foul and base as I?*
*Oh, it is better far to die!*
*Swear to me now you'll fight and fight,*
*Boy, or I'll kill you here to-night. . . .*"

## DEATH IN THE ARCTIC

### III

Curse this silence soft and black!
Sting, little light, the shadows back!
Dance, little flame, with freakish glee!
Twinkle with brilliant mockery!
Glitter on ice-robed roof and floor!
Jewel the bear-skin of the door!
Gleam in my beard, illume my breath,
Blanch the clock face that times my death!
But do not pierce that murk so deep,
Where in their sleeping-bags they sleep!
But do not linger where they lie,
They who had all the luck to die! . . .

*" There is nothing more to say;*
*Let us part and go our way.*
*Since it seems we can't agree,*
*I will go across the sea.*
*Proud of heart and strong am I;*
*Not for woman will I sigh;*
*Hold my head up gay and glad:*
*You can find another lad. . . .*

## IV

Above the igloo piteous flies
Our frayed flag to the frozen skies.
Oh, would you know how earth can be
A hell — go north of Eighty-three!
Go, scan the snows day after day,
And hope for help, and pray and pray;
Have seal-hide and sea-lice to eat;
Melt water with your body's heat;
Sleep all the fell, black winter through
Beside the dear, dead men you knew.
(The walrus blubber flares and gleams —
O God! how long a minute seems!) .  .

*"Mary, many a day has passed,*
*Since that morn of hot-head youth.*
*Come I back at last, at last,*
*Crushed with knowing of the truth;*
*How through bitter, barren years*
*You loved me, and me alone;*
*Waited, wearied, wept your tears —*
*Oh, could I atone, atone,*
*I would pay a million-fold!*
*Pay you for the love you gave.*
*Mary, look down as of old —*
*I am kneeling by your grave."*  .  .

### V

Olaf, the Blonde, was first to go;
Bitten his eyes were by the snow;
Sightless and sealed his eyes of blue,
So that he died before I knew.
Here in those poor weak arms he died:
"Wolves will not get you, lad," I lied;
"For I will watch till Spring come round;
Slumber you shall beneath the ground."
Oh, how I lied! I scarce can wait:
Strike, little clock, the hour of eight! . . .

*"Comrade, can you blame me quite?*
*The horror of the long, long night*
*Is on me, and I've borne with pain*
*So long, and hoped for help in vain.*
*So frail am I, and blind and dazed;*
*With scurvy sick, with silence crazed.*
*Beneath the Arctic's heel of hate,*
*Avid for Death I wait, I wait.*
*Oh if I falter, fail to fight,*
*Can you, dear comrade, blame me quite?"* . . .

## VI

Big Eric gave up months ago.
But seldom do men suffer so.
His feet sloughed off, his fingers died,
His hands shrunk up and mummified.
I had to feed him like a child;
Yet he was valiant, joked and smiled,
Talked of his wife and little one
(Thanks be to God that I have none),
Passed in the night without a moan,
Passed, and I'm here, alone, alone. . .

*"I've got to kill you, Dick.*
*Your life for mine, you know.*
*Better to do it quick,*
*A swift and sudden blow.*
*See! here's my hand to lick;*
*A hug before you go —*
*God! but it makes me sick:*
*Old dog, I love you so.*
*Forgive, forgive me, Dick —*
*A swift and sudden blow. . . .*

## VII

Often I start up in the dark,
Thinking the sound of bells to hear.
Often I wake from sleep: "Oh, hark!
Help . . . it is coming . . . near and
    near."
Blindly I reel toward the door;
There the snow billows bleak and bare;
Blindly I seek my den once more,
Silence and darkness and despair.
Oh, it is all a dreadful dream!
Scurvy and cold and death and dearth;
I will awake to warmth and gleam,
Silvery seas and greening earth.
Life is a dream, its wakening,
Death, gentle shadow of God's wing. . . .

*" Tick, little clock, my life away!*
  *Even a second seems a day.*
  *Even a minute seems a year,*
  *Peopled with ghosts, that press and peer*
  *Into my face so charnel white,*
  *Lit by the devilish, dancing light.*
  *Tick, little clock! mete out my fate:*
  *Tortured and tense I wait, I wait. . . ."*

## VIII

Oh, I have sworn! the hour is nigh:
When it strikes eight, I die, I die.
Raise up the gun — it stings my brow —
When it strikes eight . . . all ready . . .
    *now* —

      *      \*      \*      \**

Down from my hand the weapon dropped;
Wildly I stared. . . .
    THE CLOCK HAD STOPPED.

## IX

Phantoms and fears and ghosts have gone.
Peace seems to nestle in my brain.
Lo! the clock stopped, I'm living on;
Heart-sick I was, and less than sane.
Yet do I scorn the thing I planned,
Hearing a voice: " O coward, fight! "
Then the clock stopped . . . whose was the
    hand?
Maybe 'twas God's — ah well, all's right.
Heap on me darkness, fold on fold!
Pain! wrench and rack me! What care I?
Leap on me, hunger, thirst and cold!
I will await my time to die;
Looking to Heaven that shines above;
Looking to God, and love . . . and love.

Hark! what is that? Bells, dogs again!
Is it a dream? I sob and cry.
See! the door opens, fur-clad men
Rush to my rescue; frail am I;
Feeble and dying, dazed and glad.
There is the pistol where it dropped.
"Boys, it was hard — but I'm not mad. . . .
Look at the clock — it stopped, it stopped.
Carry me out. The heavens smile.
See! there's an arch of gold above.
Now, let me rest a little while —
*Looking to God and love . . . and love. . . .*

## DREAMS ARE BEST

I JUST think that dreams are best,
    Just to sit and fancy things;
Give your gold no acid test,
Try not how your silver rings;
Fancy women pure and good,
    Fancy men upright and true:
    Fortressed in your solitude,
Let Life be a dream to you.

For I think that Thought is all;
    Truth's a minion of the mind;
    Love's ideal comes at call;
As ye seek so shall ye find.
But ye must not seek too far;
    Things are never what they seem:
    Let a star be just a star,
And a woman — just a dream.

O you Dreamers, proud and pure,
    You have gleaned the sweet of life!
    Golden truths that shall endure
Over pain and doubt and strife.

## DREAMS ARE BEST

I would rather be a fool
    Living in my Paradise,
    Than the leader of a school,
Sadly sane and weary wise.

O you Cynics with your sneers,
    Fallen brains and hearts of brass,
    Tweak me by my foolish ears,
Write me down a simple ass!
I'll believe the real " you "
    Is the " you " without a taint;
    I'll believe each woman too,
But a slightly damaged saint.

Yes, I'll smoke my cigarette,
    Vestured in my garb of dreams,
    And I'll borrow no regret;
All is gold that golden gleams.
So I'll charm my solitude
    With the faith that Life is blest,
    Brave and noble, bright and good, ⸱ ⸱ ⸱
    Oh, I think that dreams are best!

# THE QUITTER

WHEN you're lost in the Wild, and you're scared
    as a child,
  And Death looks you bang in the eye,
And you're sore as a boil, it's according to Hoyle
  To cock your revolver and . . . die.
But the Code of a Man says: " Fight all you can,"
  And self-dissolution is barred.
In hunger and woe, oh, it's easy to blow . . .
  It's the hell-served-for-breakfast that's hard.

"You're sick of the game!" Well, now, that's a shame.
  You're young and you're brave and you're bright.
"You've had a raw deal!" I know — but don't squeal,
  Buck up, do your damnedest, and fight.
It's the plugging away that will win you the day,
  So don't be a piker, old pard!
Just draw on your grit; it's so easy to quit:
  It's the keeping-your-chin-up that's hard.

It's easy to cry that you're beaten — and die;
  It's easy to crawfish and crawl;
But to fight and to fight when hope's out of sight —
  Why, that's the best game of them all!

## THE QUITTER

And though you come out of each gruelling bout,
    All broken and beaten and scarred,
Just have one more try — it's dead easy to die,
    It's the keeping-on-living that's hard.

## THE COW JUICE CURE

THE clover was in blossom, an' the year was at the June,
When Flap-jack Billy hit the town, likewise O'Flynn's saloon.
The frost was on the fodder an' the wind was growin' keen,
When Billy got to seein' snakes in Sullivan's shebeen.

Then in meandered Deep-hole Dan, once comrade of the cup:
" Oh Billy, for the love of Mike, why don't ye sober up?
I've got the gorgus recipay, 'tis smooth an' slick as silk —
Jest quit yer strangle-holt on hooch, an' irrigate with milk.
Lackteal flooid is the lubrication you require;
Yer nervus frame-up's like a bunch of snarled piano wire.
You want to get it coated up with addypose tishoo,
So's it will work elastic-like, an' milk's the dope for you."

Well, Billy was complyable, an' in a month it's strange,
That cow-juice seemed to oppyrate a most amazin' change.

91

"Call up the water-wagon, Dan, an' book my seat,"
    sez he.

"'Tis mighty queer," sez Deep-hole Dan, "'twas just the
    same with me."

They shanghaied little Tim O'Shane, they cached him
    safe away,

An' though he objurgated some, they "cured" him night
    an' day;

An' pretty soon there came the change amazin' to explain:

"I'll never take another drink," sez Timothy O'Shane.

They tried it out on Spike Muldoon, that toper of renown;

They put it over Grouch McGraw, the terror of the
    town.

They roped in "tanks" from far and near, an' every test
    was sure,

An' like a flame there ran the fame of Deep-hole's Cow-
    juice Cure.


"It's mighty queer," sez Deep-hole Dan, "I'm puzzled
    through and through;

It's only milk from Riley's ranch, no other milk will do."

An' it jest happened on that night with no predictive plan,

He left some milk from Riley's ranch a-settin' in a pan;

An' picture his amazement when he poured that milk
    next day —

There in the bottom of the pan a dozen "colours" lay.

"Well, what d'ye know 'bout that," sez Dan; " Gosh ding
    my dasted eyes,
We've been an' had the Gold Cure, Bill, an' none of us
    was wise.
The milk's free-millin' that's a cinch; there's colours
    everywhere.
Now, let us figger this thing out — how does the dust
    git there?
' Gold from the grass-roots down,' they say — why, Bill!
    we've got it cold —
Them cows what nibbles up the grass, jest nibbles up the
    gold.
We're blasted, bloomin' millionaires; dissemble an' lie
    low:
We'll follow them gold-bearin' cows, an' prospect where
    they go."

An' so it came to pass, fer weeks them miners might be
    found
A-sneakin' round on Riley's ranch, an' snipin' at the
    ground;
Till even Riley stops an' stares, an' presently allows:
"Them boys appear to take a mighty interest in cows."
An' night an' day they shadowed each auriferous bovine,
An' panned the grass-roots on their trail, yet nivver gold
    they seen.

An' all that season, secret-like, they worked an' nothin'
    found;

An' there was colours in the milk, but none was in the
    ground.

An' mighty desperate was they, an' down upon their luck,

When sudden, inspirationlike, the source of it they struck.

An' where d'ye think they traced it too? it grieves my
    heart to tell —

In the black sand at the bottom of that wicked milkman's
    *well.*

## WHILE THE BANNOCK BAKES

**L**IGHT up your pipe again, old chum, and sit awhile
     with me;
I've got to watch the bannock bake — how restful is the
    air!
You'd little think that we were somewhere north of
    Sixty-three,
Though where I don't exactly know, and don't precisely
    care.
The man-size mountains palisade us round on every side;
The river is a-flop with fish, and ripples silver-clear;
The midnight sunshine brims yon cleft — we think it's
    the Divide;
We'll get there in a month, maybe, or maybe in a year.


It doesn't matter, does it, pal?  We're of that breed of
    men
With whom the world of wine and cards and women dis-
    agree;
Your trouble was a roofless game of poker now and then,
And " raising up my elbow," that's what got away
    with me.

We're merely " Undesirables," artistic more or less;
My horny hands are Chopin-wise; you quote your Browning well;
And yet we're fooling round for gold in this damned wilderness:
The joke is, if we found it, we would both go straight to hell.


Well, maybe we won't find it — and at least we've got the " life."
We're both as brown as berries, and could wrestle with a bear:
(That bannock's raising nicely, pal; just jab it with your knife.)
Fine specimens of manhood they would reckon us out there.
It's the tracking and the packing and the poling in the sun;
It's the sleeping in the open, it's the rugged, unfaked food;
It's the snow-shoe and the paddle, and the campfire and the gun,
And when I think of what I was, I know that it is good.

Just think of how we've poled all day up this strange
    little stream;
Since life began no eye of man has seen this place before;
How fearless all the wild things are! the banks with
    goose-grass gleam,
And there's a bronzy musk-rat sitting sniffing at his door.
A mother duck with brood of ten comes squattering along;
The tawny, white-winged ptarmigan are flying all about;
And in that swirly, golden pool, a restless, gleaming
    throng,
The trout are waiting till we condescend to take them out.


Ah, yes, it's good! I'll bet that there's no doctor like
    the Wild:
(Just turn that bannock over there; it's getting nicely
    brown.)
I might be in my grave by now, forgotten and reviled,
Or rotting like a sickly cur in some far, foreign town.
I might be that vile thing I was,— it all seems like a
    dream;
I owed a man a grudge one time that only life could pay;
And yet it's half-forgotten now — how petty these things
    seem!
(But that's "another story," pal; I'll tell it you some
    day.)

How strange two "irresponsibles" should chum away
    up here!
But round the Arctic Circle friends are few and far
    between.
We've shared the same camp-fire and tent for nigh on
    seven year,
And never had a word that wasn't cheering and serene.
We've halved the toil and split the spoil, and borne each
    other's packs;
By all the Wild's freemasonry we're brothers, tried and
    true;
We've swept on danger side by side, and fought it back
    to back,
And you would die for me, old pal, and I would die
    for you.

Now there was that time I got lost in Rory Bory Land,
(How quick the blizzards sweep on one across that
    Polar sea!)
You formed a rescue crew of One, and saw a frozen hand
That stuck out of a drift of snow — and, partner, it
    was Me.
But I got even, did I not, that day the paddle broke?
White water on the Coppermine — a rock — a split
    canoe —
Two fellows struggling in the foam (one couldn't swim
    a stroke):

## WHILE THE BANNOCK BAKES

A half-drowned man I dragged ashore . . . and
 partner, it was You.

   \*  \*  \*  \*  \*

In Rory Borealis Land the winter's long and black.
The silence seems a solid thing, shot through with wolfish
 woe;
And rowelled by the eager stars the skies vault vastly
 back,
And man seems but a little mite on that weird-lit plateau.
No thing to do but smoke and yarn of wild and mis-
 spent lives,
Beside the camp-fire there we sat — what tales you told
 to me
Of love and hate, and chance and fate, and temporary
 wives!
In Rory Borealis Land, beside the Arctic Sea.

One yarn you told me in those days I can remember still;
It seemed as if I visioned it, so sharp you sketched it in;
Bellona was the name, I think; a coast town in Brazil,
Where nobody did anything but serenade and sin.
I saw it all — the jewelled sea, the golden scythe of sand,
The stately pillars of the palms, the feathery bamboo,
The red-roofed houses and the swart, sun-dominated land,
The people ever children, and the heavens ever blue.

You told me of that girl of yours, that blossom of old
    Spain,
All glamour, grace and witchery, all passion, verve and
    glow.
How maddening she must have been!  You made me see
    her plain,
There by our little camp-fire, in the silence and the snow.
You loved her and she loved you.  She'd a husband, too,
    I think,
A doctor chap, you told me, whom she treated like a dog,
A white man living on the beach, a hopeless slave to
    drink —
(Just turn that bannock over there, that's propped
    against the log.)

That story seemed to strike me, pal — it happens every
    day:
You had to go away awhile, then somehow it befell
The doctor chap discovered, gave her up, and disappeared;
You came back, tired of her in time . . . there's
    nothing more to tell.
Hist! see those willows silvering where swamp and river
    meet!
Just reach me up my rifle quick; that's Mister Moose, I
    know —

There now, *I've got him dead to rights* . . . but
    hell! we've lots to eat
I don't believe in taking life — we'll let the beggar go.

Heigh ho! I'm tired; the bannock's cooked; it's time we
    both turned in.
The morning mist is coral-kissed, the morning sky is gold.
The camp-fire's a confessional — what funny yarns we
    spin!
It sort of made me think a bit, that story that you told.
The fig-leaf belt and Rory Bory are such odd extremes,
Yet after all how very small this old world seems to
    be . . .
Yes, that was quite a yarn, old pal, and yet to me it
    seems
You missed the point: the point is that the " doctor chap "
    . . . was ME. . . .

## THE LOST MASTER

"AND when I come to die," he said,
   "Ye shall not lay me out in state,
Nor leave your laurels at my head,
Nor cause your men of speech orate;
No monument your gift shall be,
No column in the Hall of Fame;
But just this line ye grave for me:
       "He played the game."

So when his glorious task was done,
It was not of his fame we thought;
It was not of his battles won,
But of the pride with which he fought;
But of his zest, his ringing laugh,
His trenchant scorn of praise or blame:
And so we graved his epitaph,
       "He played the game."

And so we, too, in humbler ways
Went forth to fight the fight anew,
And heeding neither blame nor praise,
We held the course he set us true.
And we, too, find the fighting sweet;

And we, too, fight for fighting's sake;
And though we go down in defeat,
And though our stormy hearts may break,
We will not do our Master shame:
We'll play the game, please God,
　　　We'll play the game.

## LITTLE MOCCASINS

COME out, O Little Moccasins, and frolic on the
 snow!
Come out, O tiny beaded feet, and twinkle in the light!
I'll play the old Red River reel, you used to love it so:
Awake, O Little Moccasins, and dance for me to-night!

Your hair was all a gleamy gold, your eyes a corn-flower
 blue;
Your cheeks were pink as tinted shells, you stepped light
 as a fawn;
Your mouth was like a coral bud, with seed pearls peep-
 ing through;
As gladdening as Spring you were, as radiant as dawn.

Come out, O Little Moccasins! I'll play so soft and
 low,
The songs you loved, the old heart-songs that in my
 mem'ry ring;

## LITTLE MOCCASINS

O child, I want to hear you now beside the campfire
    glow!
With all your heart a-throbbing in the simple words
    you sing.


For there was only you and I, and you were all to me;
And round us were the barren lands, but little did we
    fear;
Of all God's happy, happy folks the happiest were
    we. . . .
(Oh, call her, poor old fiddle mine, and maybe she will
    hear!)


Your mother was a half-breed Cree, but you were white
    all through;
And I, your father was — but well, that's neither here
    nor there;
I only know, my little Queen, that all my world was you,
And now that world can end to-night, and I will never
    care.


For there's a tiny wooden cross that pricks up through
    the snow:
(Poor little Moccasins! you're tired, and so you lie at
    rest.)

And there's a grey-haired, weary man beside the camp-
    fire glow:
(O fiddle mine! the tears to-night are drumming on
    your breast.)

## THE WANDERLUST

THE Wanderlust has lured me to the seven lonely
   seas,
Has dumped me on the tailing-piles of dearth;
The Wanderlust has haled me from the morris chairs
  of ease,
Has hurled me to the ends of all the earth.
How bitterly I've cursed it, oh, the Painted Desert
  knows,
The wraithlike heights that hug the pallid plain,
The all-but-fluid silence,—yet the longing grows and
  grows,
And I've got to glut the Wanderlust again.

 Soldier, sailor, in what a plight I've been!
 Tinker, tailor, oh what a sight I've seen!
 And I'm hitting the trail in the morning, boys,
 And you won't see my heels for dust;
 For it's " all day " with you
 When you answer the cue
   Of the Wan-der-lust.

The Wanderlust has got me . . . by the belly-aching fire,
By the fever and the freezing and the pain;
By the darkness that just drowns you, by the wail of home desire,
I've tried to break the spell of it — in vain.
Life might have been a feast for me, now there are only crumbs;
In rags and tatters, beggar-wise I sit;
Yet there's no rest or peace for me, imperious it drums,
The Wanderlust, and I must follow it.


   Highway, by-way, many a mile I've done;
   Rare way, fair way, many a height I've won;
   But I'm pulling my freight in the morning, boys,
   And it's over the hills or bust;
   For there's never a cure
   When you list to the lure
         Of the Wan-der-lust.


The Wanderlust has taught me . . . it has whispered to my heart
Things all you stay-at-homes will never know.
The white man and the savage are but three short days apart,

## THE WANDERLUST

Three days of cursing, crawling, doubt and woe.
Then it's down to chewing muclucs, to the water you
    can *eat,*
To fish you bolt with nose held in your hand.
When you get right down to cases, it's King's Grub that
    rules the races,
And the Wanderlust will help you understand.


Haunting, taunting, that is the spell of it;
Mocking, baulking, that is the hell of it;
But I'll shoulder my pack in the morning, boys,
And I'm going because I must;
For it's so-long to all
When you answer the call
            Of the Wan-der-lust.


The Wanderlust has blest me . . . in a ragged
    blanket curled,
I've watched the gulf of Heaven foam with stars;
I've walked with eyes wide open to the wonder of the
    world,
I've seen God's flood of glory burst its bars.
I've seen the gold a-blinding in the riffles of the sky,
Till I fancied me a bloated plutocrat;

But I'm freedom's happy bond-slave, and I will be till
    I die,
And I've got to thank the Wanderlust for that.


  Wild heart, child heart, all of the world your home.
  Glad heart, mad heart, what can you do but roam?
  Oh, I'll beat it once more in the morning, boys,
  With a pinch of tea and a crust;
  For you cannot deny
  When you hark to the cry
       Of the Wan-der-lust.


The Wanderlust will claim me at the finish for its own.
I'll turn my back on men and face the Pole.
Beyond the Arctic outposts I will venture all alone;
Some Never-never Land will be my goal.
Thank God! there's none will miss me, for I've been a
    bird of flight;
And in my moccasins I'll take my call;
For the Wanderlust has ruled me,
And the Wanderlust has schooled me,
And I'm ready for the darkest trail of all.

## THE WANDERLUST

Grim land, dim land, oh, how the vastness calls!
Far land, star land, oh, how the stillness falls!
For you never can tell if it's heaven or hell,
And I'm taking the trail on trust;
But I haven't a doubt
That my soul will leap out
        On its Wan-der-lust.

## THE TRAPPER'S CHRISTMAS EVE

IT'S mighty lonesome-like and drear.
  Above the Wild the moon rides high,
And shows up sharp and needle-clear
The emptiness of earth and sky;
No happy homes with love a-glow;
No Santa Claus to make believe:
Just snow and snow, and then more snow;
It's Christmas Eve, it's Christmas Eve.

And here am I where all things end,
And Undesirables are hurled;
A poor old man without a friend,
Forgot and dead to all the world;
Clean out of sight and out of mind . . .
Well, maybe it is better so;
We all in life our level find,
And mine, I guess, is pretty low.

Yet as I sit with pipe alight
Beside the cabin-fire, it's queer
This mind of mine must take to-night
The backward trail of fifty year.

## THE TRAPPER'S CHRISTMAS EVE

The school-house and the Christmas tree;
The children with their cheeks a-glow;
Two bright blue eyes that smile on me ₒ ₒ ₒ
Just half a century ago.

Again (it's maybe forty years),
With faith and trust almost divine,
These same blue eyes, abrim with tears,
Through depths of love look into mine.
A parting, tender, soft and low,
With arms that cling and lips that cleave . ₒ
Ah me! it's all so long ago,
Yet seems so sweet this Christmas Eve.

Just thirty years ago, again . . .
We say a bitter, *last* good-bye;
Our lips are white with wrath and pain;
Our little children cling and cry.
Whose was the fault? it matters not,
For man and woman both deceive;
It's buried now and all forgot,
Forgiven, too, this Christmas Eve.

And she (God pity me) is dead;
Our children men and women grown.
I like to think that they are wed,
With little children of their own,

That crowd around their Christmas tree . . .
I would not ever have them grieve,
Or shed a single tear for me,
To mar their joy this Christmas Eve.

Stripped to the buff and gaunt and still
Lies all the land in grim distress.
Like lost soul wailing, long and shrill,
A wolf-howl cleaves the emptiness.
Then hushed as Death is everything.
The moon rides haggard and forlorn . . .
"O hark the herald angels sing!"
God bless all men — it's Christmas morn.

## THE WORLD'S ALL RIGHT

*B*E *honest, kindly, simple, true;*
  *Seek good in all, scorn but pretence;*
*Whatever sorrow come to you,*
*Believe in Life's Beneficence!*

The World's all right; serene I sit,
And cease to puzzle over it.
There's much that's mighty strange, no doubt;
But Nature knows what she's about;
And in a million years or so
We'll know more than to-day we know.
Old Evolution's under way —
      What ho! the World's all right, I say.

Could things be other than they are?
All's in its place, from mote to star.
The thistledown that flits and flies
Could drift no hair-breadth otherwise.
What is, must be; with rhythmic laws
All Nature chimes, Effect and Cause.
The sand-grain and the sun obey —
      What ho! the World's all right, I say.

## THE WORLD'S ALL RIGHT

Just try to get the Cosmic touch,
The sense that " you " don't matter much.
A million stars are in the sky;
A million planets plunge and die;
A million million men are sped;
A million million wait ahead.
Each plays his part and has his day —
      What ho! the World's all right, I say.

Just try to get the Chemic view:
A million million lives made " you."
In lives a million you will be
Immortal down Eternity;
Immortal on this earth to range,
With never death, but ever change.
You always were, and will be aye —
      What ho! the World's all right, I say.

Be glad!  And do not blindly grope
For Truth that lies beyond our scope:
A sober plot informeth all
Of Life's uproarious carnival.
Your day is such a little one,
A gnat that lives from sun to sun;
Yet gnat and you have parts to play —
      What ho! the World's all right, I say.

# THE WORLD'S ALL RIGHT

And though it's written from the start,
Just act your best your little part.
Just be as happy as you can,
And serve your kind, and die — a man.
Just live the good that in you lies,
And seek no guerdon of the skies;
Just make your Heaven here, to-day —
      What ho! the World's all right, I say.

Remember! in Creation's swing
The Race and not the man's the thing.
There's battle, murder, sudden death,
And pestilence, with poisoned breath.
Yet quick forgotten are such woes;
On, on the stream of Being flows.
Truth, Beauty, Love uphold their sway —
      What ho! the World's all right, I say.

The World's all right; serene I sit,
And joy that I am part of it;
And put my trust in Nature's plan,
And try to aid her all I can;
Content to pass, if in my place
I've served the uplift of the Race.
Truth! Beauty! Love! O Radiant Day —
      What ho! the World's all right, I say.

## THE BALDNESS OF CHEWED EAR

WHEN Chewed-ear Jenkins got hitched up to
    Guinneyveer McGee,
His flowin' locks, ye recollect, wuz frivolous an' free;
But in old Hymen's jack-pot, it's a most amazin' thing,
Them flowin' locks jest disappeared like snow-balls in
    the Spring;
Jest seemed to wilt an' fade away like dead leaves in
    the Fall,
An' left old Chewed-ear balder than a white-washed can-
    non ball.

Now Missis Chewed-ear Jenkins, that wuz Guinneyveer
    McGee,
Wuz jest about as fine a draw as ever made a pair;
But when the boys got joshin' an' suggested it was she
That must be inflooenshul for the old man's slump in
    hair —
Why! Missis Chewed-ear Jenkins jest went clean up
    in the air.

" To demonstrate," sez she that night, " the lovin' wife
    I am,
I've bought a dozen bottles of Bink's Anty-Dandruff
    Balm.
'Twill make yer hair jest sprout an' curl like squash·
    vines in the sun,
An' I'm propose to sling it on till every drop is done."
That hit old Chewed-ear's funny side, so he lays back
    an' hollers:
" The day you raise a hair, old girl, you'll git a thou-
    sand dollars."


Now, whether 'twas the prize or not 'tis mighty hard
    to say,
But Chewed-ear didn't seem to have much comfort from
    that day.
With bottles of that dandruff dope she followed at his
    heels,
An' sprinkled an' massaged him even when he ate his
    meals.
She waked him from his beauty sleep with tender, lovin'
    care.
An' rubbed an' scrubbed assiduous, yet never sign of hair.

Well, naturally all the boys soon tumbled to the joke,
An' at the Wow-wow's Social 'twas Cold-deck Davis
  spoke:
" The little woman's working mighty hard on Chewed-
  ear's crown;
Let's give her for a three-fifth's share a hundred dollars
  down.
We stand to make five hundred clear — boys, drink in
  whiskey straight:
' The Chewed-ear Jenkins Hirsute Propagation Syndicate.' "


The boys wuz on, an' soon chipped in the necessary dust;
They primed up a committy to negotiate the deal;
Then Missis Jenkins yielded, bein' rather in disgust,
An' all wuz signed an' witnessed, an' invested with a seal.
They rounded up old Chewed-ear, an' they broke it what
  they'd done;
Allowed they'd bought an interest in his chance of raisin'
  hair;
They yanked his hat off anxiouslike, opinin' one by one
Their magnifyin' glasses showed fine prospects every-
  where.
They bought Hairlene, an' Thatchem, an' Jay's Capil-
  lery Juice,

An' Seven Something Sisters, an' Macassar an' Bay Rum,
An' everyone insisted on his speshul right to sluice
His speshul line of lotion onto Chewed-ear's cranium.
They only got the merrier the more the old man roared,
An' shares in " Jenkins Hirsute " went sky-highin' on
    the board.


The Syndicate wuz hopeful that they'd demonstrate the
    pay,
An' Missis Jenkins laboured in her perseverin' way.
The boys discussed on " surface rights," an' " out-crops "
    an' so on,
An' planned to have it " crown " surveyed, an' blue prints
    of it drawn.
They ran a base line, sluiced an' yelled, an' everyone wuz
    glad,
Except the balance of the property, an' he wuz " mad."
" It gives me pain," he interjects, " to squash yer glowin'
    dream,
But you wuz fools when you got in on this here ' Hir-
    sute ' scheme.
You'll never raise a hair on me," when lo! that very
    night,
Preparin' to retire he got a most onpleasant fright:
For on that shinin' dome of his, so prominently bare,
He felt the baby outcrop of a second growth of hair.

A thousand dollars! Sufferin' Cæsar! Well, it must
    be saved!

He grabbed his razor recklesslike, an' shaved an' shaved
    an' shaved.

An' when his head was smooth again he gives a mighty
    sigh,

An' sneaks away, an' buys some Hair Destroyer on the
    sly.

So there wuz Missis Jenkins with "Restorer" wagin'
    fight,

An' Chewed-ear with "Destroyer" circumventin' her at
    night.

The battle wuz a mighty one; his nerves wuz on the
    strain,

An' yet in spite of all he did that hair began to gain.

The situation grew intense, so quietly one day,

He gave his share-holders the slip, an' made his get-
    a-way.

Jest like a criminal he skipped, an' aimed to defalcate

The Chewed-ear Jenkins Hirsute Propagation Syndicate.

His guilty secret burned him, an' he sought the city's din:

"I've got to get a wig," sez he, "to cover up my sin.

It's growin', growin' night an' day; it's most amazin'
    hair";

An' when he looked at it that night, he shuddered with
    despair.

He shuddered an' suppressed a cry at what his optics
    seen —
For on my word of honour, boys, that hair wuz growin'
    *green*.

At first he guessed he'd get some dye, an' try to dye
    it black;
An' then he saw 'twas Nemmysis wuz layin' on his track.
He must jest face the music, an' confess the thing he
    done,
An' pay the boys an' Guinneyveer the money they had
    won.
An' then there came a big idee — it thrilled him like
    a shock.
Why not control the Syndicate by buyin' up the Stock?

An' so next day he hurried back with smoothly shaven
    pate,
An' for a hundred dollars he bought up the Syndicate.
'Twas mighty frenzied finance an' the boys set up a roar,
But " Hirsutes " from the market wuz withdrawn for
    evermore.
An' to this day in Nuggetsville they tell the tale how
    slick
The Syndicate sold out too soon, and Chewed-ear turned
    the trick.

## THE MOTHER

THERE will be a singing in your heart,
　　There will be a rapture in your eyes;
You will be a woman set apart,
You will be so wonderful and wise.
You will sleep, and when from dreams you start,
As of one that wakes in Paradise,
There will be a singing in your heart,
There will be a rapture in your eyes.

There will be a moaning in your heart,
There will be an anguish in your eyes;
You will see your dearest ones depart,
You will hear their quivering good-byes.
Yours will be the heart-ache and the smart,
Tears that scald and lonely sacrifice;
There will be a moaning in your heart,
There will be an anguish in your eyes.

There will come a glory in your eyes,
There will come a peace within your heart;
Sitting 'neath the quiet evening skies,
Time will dry the tear and dull the smart.

## THE MOTHER

You will know that you have played your part;
Yours shall be the love that never dies:
You, with Heaven's peace within your heart,
You, with God's own glory in your eyes.

## THE DREAMER

THE lone man gazed and gazed upon his gold,
　　His sweat, his blood, the wage of weary days;
But now how sweet, how doubly sweet to hold
All gay and gleamy to the campfire blaze.
The evening sky was sinister and cold;
The willows shivered, wanly lay the snow;
The uncommiserating land, so old,
So worn, so grey, so niggard in its woe,
Peered through its ragged shroud.　The lone man sighed,
Poured back the gaudy dust into its poke,
Gazed at the seething river listless-eyed,
Loaded his corn-cob pipe as if to smoke;
Then crushed with weariness and hardship crept
Into his ragged robe, and swiftly slept.

． 　． 　． 　． 　． 　． 　．

Hour after hour went by; a shadow slipped
From vasts of shadow to the camp-fire flame;
Gripping a rifle with a deadly aim,
A gaunt and hairy man with wolfish eyes ． ． ，

＊ 　＊ 　＊ 　＊ 　＊

## THE DREAMER

The sleeper dreamed, and lo! this was his dream:
He rode a streaming horse across a moor.
Sudden 'mid pit-black night a lightning gleam
Showed him a way-side inn, forlorn and poor.
A sullen host unbarred the creaking door,
And led him to a dim and dreary room;
Wherein he sat and poked the fire a-roar,
So that weird shadows jigged athwart the gloom.
He ordered wine. 'Od's blood! but he was tired.
What matter! Charles was crushed and George was
    King;
His party high in power; how he aspired!
Red guineas packed his purse, too tight to ring.
The fire-light gleamed upon his silken hose,
His silver buckles and his powdered wig.
What ho! more wine! He drank, he slowly rose.
What made the shadows dance that madcap jig?
He clutched the candle, steered his way to bed,
And in a trice was sleeping like the dead.

   o     .     .     .     .     .     .

Across the room there crept, so shadow soft,
His sullen host, with naked knife a-gleam,
(A gaunt and hairy man with wolfish eyes.) . .
And as he lay, the sleeper dreamed a dream.
    *       *       *       *       *

## THE DREAMER

'Twas in a ruder land, a wilder day.
A rival princeling sat upon his throne,
Within a dungeon, dark and foul he lay,
With chains that bit and festered to the bone.
They haled him harshly to a vaulted room,
Where One gazed on him with malignant eye;
And in that devil-face he read his doom,
Knowing that ere the dawn-light he must die.
Well, he was sorrow-glutted; let them bring
Their prize assassins to the bloody work.
His kingdom lost, yet would he die a King,
Fearless and proud, as when he faced the Turk.
Ah God! the glory of that great Crusade!
The bannered pomp, the gleam, the splendid urge!
The crash of reeking combat, blade to blade!
The reeling ranks, blood-avid and a-surge!
For long he thought; then feeling o'er him creep
Vast weariness, he fell into a sleep.

    .     .     .     .     .     .     .

The cell door opened; soft the headsman came,
Within his hand a mighty axe a-gleam,
(A gaunt and hairy man with wolfish eyes,)  . . .
And as he lay, the sleeper dreamed a dream.
    *      *      *      *      *

# THE DREAMER

'Twas in a land unkempt of life's red dawn;
Where in his sanded cave he dwelt alone;
Sleeping by day, or sometimes worked upon
His flint-head arrows and his knives of stone;
By night stole forth and slew the savage boar,
So that he loomed a hunter of loud fame,
And many a skin of wolf and wild-cat wore,
And counted many a flint-head to his name;
Wherefore he walked the envy of the band,
Hated and feared, but matchless in his skill.
Till lo! one night deep in that shaggy land,
He tracked a yearling bear and made his kill;
Then over-worn he rested by a stream,
And sank into a sleep too deep for dream.

   .     .     .     .     .     .     .

Hunting his food a rival caveman crept
Through those dark woods, and marked him where he
    lay;
Cowered and crawled upon him as he slept,
Poising a mighty stone aloft to slay —
(A gaunt and hairy man with wolfish eyes.)  .  .  .

      *       *       *       *       *

# THE DREAMER

The great stone crashed.  The Dreamer shrieked and
    woke,
And saw, fear-blinded, in his dripping cell,
A gaunt and hairy man, who with one stroke
Swung a great ax of steel that flashed and fell . . .

So that he woke amid his bedroom gloom,
And saw, hair-poised, a naked, thirsting knife,
A gaunt and hairy man with eyes of doom —
And then the blade plunged down to drink his life . . .
So that he woke, wrenched back his robe, and looked,
And saw beside his dying fire upstart
A gaunt and hairy man with finger crooked —
A rifle rang, a bullet searched his heart . . .

    *      *      *      *      *

The morning sky was sinister and cold.
Grotesque the Dreamer sprawled, and did not rise
For long and long there gazed upon some gold
*A gaunt and hairy man with wolfish eyes.*

## AT THIRTY-FIVE

THREE score and ten, the psalmist saith,
   And half my course is well-nigh run;
I've had my flout at dusty death,
I've had my whack of feast and fun.
I've mocked at those who prate and preach;
I've laughed with any man alive;
But now with sobered heart I reach
The Great Divide of Thirty-five.

And looking back I must confess
I've little cause to feel elate.
I've played the mummer more or less;
I fumbled fortune, flouted fate.
I've vastly dreamed and little done;
I've idly watched my brothers strive:
Oh, I have loitered in the sun
By primrose paths to Thirty-five!

And those who matched me in the race,
Well, some are out and trampled down;
The others jog with sober pace;
Yet one wins delicate renown.

O midnight feast and famished dawn!
O gay, hard life, with hope alive!
O golden youth, forever gone,
How sweet you seem at Thirty-five!

Each of our lives is just a book
As absolute as Holy Writ;
We humbly read, and may not look
Ahead, nor change one word of it.
And here are joys and here are pains;
And here we fail and here we thrive;
O wondrous volume! what remains
When we reach chapter Thirty-five?

The very best, I dare to hope,
Ere Fate writes Finis to the tome;
A wiser head, a wider scope,
And for the gipsy heart, a home;
A songful home, with loved ones near,
With joy, with sunshine all alive:
Watch me grow younger every year—
Old Age! thy name is Thirty-five!

## THE SQUAW MAN

THE cow-moose comes to water, and the beaver's
  overbold,
The net is in the eddy of the stream;
The teepee stars the vivid sward with russet, red and
  gold,
And in the velvet gloom the fire's a-gleam.
The night is ripe with quiet, rich with incense of the
  pine;
From sanctuary lake I hear the loon;
The peaks are bright against the blue, and drenched
  with sunset wine,
And like a silver bubble is the moon.


Cloud-high I climbed but yesterday; a hundred miles
  around
I looked to see a rival fire a-gleam.
As in a crystal lens it lay, a land without a bound,
All lure, and virgin vastitude, and dream.
The great sky soared exultantly, the great earth bared
  its breast,
All river-veined and patterned with the pine;

The heedless hordes of caribou were streaming to the
    West,
A land of lustrous mystery — and mine.

Yea, mine to frame my Odyssey: Oh, little do they know
My conquest and the kingdom that I keep!
The meadows of the musk-ox, where the laughing
    grasses grow,
The rivers where the careless conies leap.
Beyond the silent Circle, where white men are fierce
    and few,
I lord it, and I mock at man-made law;
Like a flame upon the water is my little light canoe,
And yonder in the fireglow is my squaw.

A squaw man! yes, that's what I am; sneer at me if you
    will.
I've gone the grilling pace that cannot last;
With bawdry, bridge and brandy — Oh, I've drank
    enough to kill
A dozen such as you, but that is past.
I've swung round to my senses, found the place where
    I belong;
The City made a madman out of me;
But here beyond the Circle, where there's neither right
    or wrong,
I leap from life's straight-jacket, and I'm free.

Yet ever in the far forlorn, by trails of lone desire;
Yet ever in the dawn's white leer of hate;
Yet ever by the dripping kill, beside the drowsy fire,
There comes the fierce heart-hunger for a mate.
There comes the mad blood-clamour for a woman's
 clinging hand,
Love-humid eyes, the velvet of a breast;
And so I sought the Bonnet-plumes, and chose from out
 the band
The girl I thought the sweetest and the best.

O wistful women I have loved before my dark disgrace!
O women fair and rare in my home land!
Dear ladies, if I saw you now I'd turn away my face,
Then crawl to kiss your foot-prints in the sand!
And yet — that day the rifle jammed — a wounded moose
 at bay —
A roar, a charge . . . I faced it with my knife:
A shot from out the willow-scrub, and there the monster
 lay. . . .
Yes, little Laughing Eyes, you saved my life.

The man must have the woman, and we're all brutes
 more or less,
Since first the male ape shinned the family tree;
And yet I think I love her with a husband's tenderness,
And yet I know that she would die for me.

Oh, if I left you, Laughing Eyes, and nevermore came
    back,
God help you, girl! I know what you would
    do. . . .
I see the lake wan in the moon, and from the shadow
    black,
There drifts a little, *empty* birch canoe.

We're here beyond the Circle, where there's never wrong
    nor right;
We aren't spliced according to the law;
But by the gods I hail you on this hushed and holy
    night
As the mother of my children, and my squaw.
I see your little slender face set in the firelight glow;
I pray that I may never make it sad;
I hear you croon a baby song, all slumber-soft and low —
God bless you, little Laughing Eyes! I'm glad.

## HOME AND LOVE

JUST Home and Love! the words are small
    Four little letters unto each;
And yet you will not find in all
The wide and gracious range of speech
Two more so tenderly complete:
When angels talk in Heaven above,
I'm sure they have no words more sweet
    Than Home and Love.

Just Home and Love! it's hard to guess
Which of the two were best to gain;
Home without Love is bitterness;
Love without Home is often pain.
No! each alone will seldom do;
Somehow they travel hand and glove:
If you win one you must have two,
    Both Home and Love.

And if you've both, well then I'm sure
You ought to sing the whole day long;
It doesn't matter if you're poor
With these to make divine your song.

And so I praisefully repeat,
When angels talk in Heaven above,
There are no words more simply sweet
Than Home and Love.

## I'M SCARED OF IT ALL

I'M scared of it all, God's truth! so I am;
 It's too big and brutal for me.
My nerve's on the raw and I don't give a damn
For all the "hoorah" that I see.
I'm pinned between subway and overhead train,
Where automobillies swoop down:
Oh, I want to go back to the timber again —
I'm scared of the terrible town.

I want to go back to my lean, ashen plains;
My rivers that flash into foam;
My ultimate valleys where solitude reigns;
My trail from Fort Churchill to Nome.
My forests packed full of mysterious gloom,
My ice-fields agrind and aglare:
The city is deadfalled with danger and doom —
I know that I'm safer up there.

I watch the wan faces that flash in the street;
All kinds and all classes I see.
Yet never a one in the million I meet,
Has the smile of a comrade for me.

Just jaded and panting like dogs in a pack;
Just tensed and intent on the goal:
O God! but I'm lonesome — I wish I was back,
Up there in the land of the Pole.

I wish I was back on the Hunger Plateaus,
And seeking the lost caribou;
I wish I was up where the Coppermine flows
To the kick of my little canoe.
I'd like to be far on some weariful shore,
In the Land of the Blizzard and Bear;
Oh, I wish I was snug in the Arctic once more,
For I know I am safer up there!

I prowl in the canyons of dismal unrest;
I cringe — I'm so weak and so small.
I can't get my bearings, I'm crushed and oppressed
With the haste and the waste of it all.
The slaves and the madman, the lust and the sweat,
The fear in the faces I see;
The getting, the spending, the fever, the fret —
It's too bleeding cruel for me.

I feel it's all wrong, but I can't tell you why —
The palace, the hovel next door;
The insolent towers that sprawl to the sky,
The crush and the rush and the roar.

# I'M SCARED OF IT ALL

I'm trapped like a fox and I fear for my pelt;
I cower in the crash and the glare;
Oh, I want to be back in the avalanche belt,
For I know that it's safer up there!

I'm scared of it all: Oh, afar I can hear
The voice of my solitudes call!
We're nothing but brute with a little veneer,
And nature is best after all.
There's tumult and terror abroad in the street;
There's menace and doom in the air;
I've got to get back to my thousand-mile beat;
The trail where the cougar and silver-tip meet;
The snows and the camp-fire, with wolves at my feet,
　　　Good-bye, for it's safer up there.

　　　*To be forming good habits up there;*
　　　*To be starving on rabbits up there;*
　　　*In your hunger and woe,*
　　　*Though it's sixty below,*
　　　*Oh, I know that it's safer up there!*

## A SONG OF SUCCESS

HO! we were strong, we were swift, we were brave.
   Youth was a challenge, and Life was a fight.
All that was best in us gladly we gave,
Sprang from the rally, and leapt for the height.
Smiling is Love in a foam of Spring flowers:
Harden our hearts to him — on let us press!
Oh, what a triumph and pride shall be ours!
See where it beacons, the star of success!

Cares seem to crowd on us — so much to do;
New fields to conquer, and time's on the wing.
Grey hairs are showing, a wrinkle or two;
Somehow our footstep is losing its spring.
Pleasure's forsaken us, Love ceased to smile;
Youth has been funeralled; Age travels fast.
Sometimes we wonder: is it worth while?
There! we have gained to the summit at last.

Aye, we have triumphed! Now must we haste,
Revel in victory . . . why! what is wrong?
Life's choicest vintage is flat to the taste —
Are we too late? Have we laboured too long?

## A SONG OF SUCCESS

Wealth, power, fame we hold . . . ah! but the
    truth:
Would we not give this vain glory of ours
For one mad, glad year of glorious youth,
Life in the Springtide, and Love in the flowers.

## THE SONG OF THE CAMP FIRE

### I

**H**EED me, feed me, I am hungry, I am red-tongued
with desire;
Boughs of balsam, slabs of cedar, gummy fagots of the
pine,
Heap them on me, let me hug them to my eager heart
of fire,
Roaring, soaring up to heaven as a symbol and a sign.
Bring me knots of sunny maple, silver birch and
tamarack;
Leaping, sweeping, I will lap them with my ardent
wings of flame;
I will kindle them to glory, I will beat the darkness
back;
Streaming, gleaming, I will goad them to my glory and
my fame.

Bring me gnarly limbs of live-oak, aid me in my frenzied fight;
Strips of iron-wood, scaly blue-gum, writhing redly in
my hold;
With my lunge of lurid lances, with my whips that flail
the night,
They will burgeon into beauty, they will foliate in gold.

Let me star the dim sierras, stab with light the inland
    seas;
Roaming wind and roaring darkness! seek no mercy at
    my hands;
I will mock the marly heavens, lamp the purple prairies,
I will flaunt my deathless banners down the far, un-
    houseled lands.
In the vast and vaulted pine-gloom where the pillared
    forests frown,
By the sullen, bestial rivers running where God only
    knows,
On the starlit coral beaches when the combers thunder
    down,
In the death-spell of the barrens, in the shudder of the
    snows;
In a blazing belt of triumph from the palm-leaf to the
    pine,
As a symbol of defiance lo! the wilderness I span;
And my beacons burn exultant as an everlasting sign
Of unending domination, of the mastery of Man;
I, the Life, the fierce Uplifter, I that weaned him from
    the mire;
I, the angel and the devil, I, the tyrant and the slave;
I, the Spirit of the Struggle; I, the mighty God of Fire;
I, the Maker and Destroyer; I, the Giver and the
    Grave.

### II

Gather round me, boy and grey-beard, frontiersman of
every kind.

Few are you, and far and lonely, yet an army forms
behind:

By your camp-fires shall they know you, ashes scattered
to the wind.

Peer into my heart of solace, break your bannock at my
blaze;

Smoking, stretched in lazy shelter, build your castles
as you gaze;

Or, it may be, deep in dreaming, think of dim, unhappy
days.

Let my warmth and glow caress you, for your trails are
grim and hard;

Let my arms of comfort press you, hunger-hewn and
battle-scarred:

O my lovers! how I bless you with your lives so madly
marred!

For you seek the silent spaces, and their secret lore you
glean:

For you win the savage races, and the brutish Wild you
wean;

And I gladden desert places, where camp-fire has never
been.

## THE SONG OF THE CAMP FIRE

From the Pole unto the Tropics is there trail ye have
    not dared?
And because you hold death lightly, so by death shall
    you be spared,
(As the sages of the ages in their pages have declared.)

On the roaring Arkilinik in a leaky bark canoe;
Up the cloud of Mount McKinley, where the avalanche
    leaps through;
In the furnace of Death Valley, when the mirage glim-
    mers blue.

Now a smudge of wiry willows on the weary Kusko-
    quim;
Now a flare of gummy pine-knots where Vancouver's
    scaur is grim;
Now a gleam of sunny ceiba, when the Cuban beaches
    dim.

Always, always God's Great Open: lo! I burn with
    keener light
In the corridors of silence, in the vestibules of night;
'Mid the ferns and grasses gleaming, was there ever gem
    so bright?

Not for weaklings, not for women, like my brother of
the hearth;
Ring your songs of wrath around me, I was made for
manful mirth,
In the lusty, gusty greatness, on the bald spots of the
earth.

Men, my masters! men, my lovers! ye have fought and
ye have bled;
Gather round my ruddy embers, softly glowing is my
bed;
By my heart of solace dreaming, rest ye and be comforted!

### III

I am dying, O my masters! by my fitful flame ye sleep;
My purple plumes of glory droop forlorn.
Grey ashes choke and cloak me, and above the pines
there creep
The stealthy silver moccasins of morn.
There comes a countless army, it's the Legion of the
Light;
It tramps in gleaming triumph round the world;
And before its jewelled lances all the shadows of the
night
Back in to abysmal darknesses are hurled.

# THE SONG OF THE CAMP FIRE

Leap to life again, my lovers! ye must toil and never
 tire;
 The day of daring, doing, brightens clear,
When the bed of spicy cedar and the jovial camp-fire
 Must only be a memory of cheer.
There is hope and golden promise in the vast portentous
 dawn;
 There is glamour in the glad, effluent sky:
Go and leave me; I will dream of you and love you
 when you're gone;
 I have served you, O my masters! let me die.


A little heap of ashes, grey and sodden by the rain,
 Wind-scattered, blurred and blotted by the snow:
Let that be all to tell of me, and glorious again,
 Ye things of greening gladness, leap and glow!
A black scar in the sunshine by the palm-leaf or the pine,
 Blind to the night and dead to all desire;
Yet oh, of life and uplift what a symbol and a sign!
Yet oh, of power and conquest what a destiny is mine!
A little heap of ashes — Yea! a miracle divine,
 The foot-print of a god, all-radiant Fire.

## HER LETTER

"I'M taking pen in hand this night, and hard it is for
  me;
My poor old fingers tremble so, my hand is stiff and
  slow,
And even with my glasses on I'm troubled sore to
  see. . . .
You'd little know your mother, boy; you'd little, little
  know.
You mind how brisk and bright I was, how straight and
  trim and smart;
'Tis weariful I am the now, and bent and frail and grey.
I'm waiting at the road's end, lad; and all that's in my
  heart,
Is just to see my boy again before I'm called away."


"Oh well I mind the sorry day you crossed the gurly
  sea;
'Twas like the heart was torn from me, a waeful wife
  was I.
You said that you'd be home again in two years, maybe
  three;

But nigh a score of years have gone, and still the years
  go by.
I know it's cruel hard for you, you've bairnies of your
  own;
I know the siller's hard to win, and folks have used
  you ill:
But oh, think of your mother, lad, that's waiting by her
  lone!
And even if you canna come — *just write and say you
  will."*


" Aye, even though there's little hope, just promise that
  you'll try.
It's weary, weary waiting, lad; just say you'll come next
  year.
I'm thinking there will be no ' next '; I'm thinking soon
  I'll lie
With all the ones I've laid away  .  .  .  but oh, the
  hope will cheer!
You know you're all that's left to me, and we are seas
  apart;
But if you'll only *say* you'll come, then will I hope and
  pray.
I'm waiting by the grave-side, lad; and all that's in my
  heart
Is just to see my boy again before I'm called away."

## THE MAN WHO KNEW

THE Dreamer visioned Life as it might be,
   And from his dream forthright a picture grew,
A painting all the people thronged to see,
And joyed therein — till came the Man Who Knew,
Saying: " 'Tis bad!  Why do ye gape, ye fools!
He painteth not according to the schools."

The Dreamer probed Life's mystery of woe,
And in a book he sought to give the clue;
The people read, and saw that it was so,
And read again — then came the Man Who Knew,
Saying: "Ye witless ones! this book is vile:
It hath not got the rudiments of style."

Love smote the Dreamer's lips, and silver clear
He sang a song so sweet, so tender true,
That all the market-place was thrilled to hear,
And listened rapt — till came the Man Who Knew,
Saying: " His technique's wrong; he singeth ill.
Waste not your time."  The singer's voice was still.

## THE MAN WHO KNEW

And then the people roused as if from sleep,
Crying: " What care we if it be not Art!
Hath he not charmed us, made us laugh and weep?
Come, let us crown him where he sits apart."
Then, with his picture spurned, his book unread,
His song unsung, they found their Dreamer — *dead.*

## THE LOGGER

IN the moonless, misty night, with my little pipe alight,
　　I am sitting by the camp-fire's fading cheer;
Oh, the dew is falling chill on the dim, deer-haunted
　　　　hill,
　　And the breakers in the bay are moaning drear.
The toilful hours are sped, the boys are long abed,
　　And I alone a weary vigil keep;
In the sightless, sullen sky I can hear the night-hawk cry,
　　And the frogs in frenzied chorus from the creek.

And somehow the embers' glow brings me back the long
　　　　ago,
　　The days of merry laughter and light song;
When I sped the hours away with the gayest of the gay
　　In the giddy whirl of fashion's festal throng.
Oh, I ran a grilling race and I little recked the pace,
　　For the lust of youth ran riot in my blood;
But at last I made a stand in this God-forsaken land
　　Of the pine-tree and the mountain and the flood.

And now I've got to stay, with an overdraft to pay,
 For pleasure in the past with future pain;
And I'm not the chap to whine, for if the chance were
  mine
  I know I'd choose the old life once again.
With its woman's eyes a-shine, and its flood of golden
  wine;
  Its fever and its frolic and its fun;
The old life with its din, its laughter and its sin —
  And chuck me in the gutter when it's done.

Ah, well! it's past and gone, and the memory is wan,
 That conjures up each old familiar face;
And here by fortune hurled, I am dead to all the world,
  And I've learned to lose my pride and keep my
  place.
My ways are hard and rough, and my arms are strong
  and tough,
  And I hew the dizzy pine till darkness falls;
And sometimes I take a dive, just to keep my heart alive,
  Among the gay saloons and dancing halls.

In the distant, dinful town just a little drink to drown
 The cares that crowd and canker in my brain;
Just a little joy to still set my pulses all a-thrill,
  Then back to brutish labour once again.

And things will go on so until one day I shall know
    That Death has got me cinched beyond a doubt;
Then I'll crawl away from sight, and morosely in the
       night
    My weary, wasted life will peter out.

Then the boys will gather round, and they'll launch me
       in the ground,
    And pile the stones the timber wolf to foil;
And the moaning pine will wave overhead a nameless
       grave,
    Where the black snake in the sunshine loves to coil.
And they'll leave me there alone, and perhaps with
       softened tone
    Speak of me sometimes in the camp-fire's glow,
As a played-out, broken chum, who has gone to King-
       dom Come,
    And who went the pace in England long ago.

## THE PASSING OF THE YEAR

MY glass is filled, my pipe is lit,
   My den is all a cosy glow;
And snug before the fire I sit,
   And wait to *feel* the old year go.
I dedicate to solemn thought
   Amid my too-unthinking days,
This sober moment, sadly fraught
   With much of blame, with little praise.

Old Year! upon the Stage of Time
   You stand to bow your last adieu;
A moment, and the prompter's chime
   Will ring the curtain down on you.
Your mien is sad, your step is slow;
   You falter as a Sage in pain;
Yet turn, Old Year, before you go,
   And face your audience again.

That sphinx-like face, remote, austere,
   Let us all read, whate'er the cost:
O Maiden! why that bitter tear?
   Is it for dear one you have lost?

Is it for fond illusion gone?
  For trusted lover proved untrue?
O sweet girl-face, so sad, so wan
  What hath the Old Year meant to you?

And you, O neighbour on my right
  So sleek, so prosperously clad!
What see you in that aged wight
  That makes your smile so gay and glad?
What opportunity unmissed?
  What golden gain, what pride of place?
What splendid hope?  O Optimist!
  What read you in that withered face?

And You, deep shrinking in the gloom,
  What find you in that filmy gaze?
What menace of a tragic doom?
  What dark, condemning yesterdays?
What urge to crime, what evil done?
  What cold, confronting shape of fear?
O haggard, haunted, hidden One
  What see you in the dying year?

And so from face to face I flit,
  The countless eyes that stare and stare;
Some are with approbation lit,
  And some are shadowed with despair.

## THE PASSING OF THE YEAR

Some show a smile and some a frown;
  Some joy and hope, some pain and woe:
Enough!  Oh, ring the curtain down!
  Old weary year! it's time to go.

My pipe is out, my glass is dry;
  My fire is almost ashes too;
But once again, before you go,
  And I prepare to meet the New:
Old Year! a parting word that's true,
  For we've been comrades, you and I —
*I thank God for each day of you;*
  There! bless you now!  Old Year, good-bye!

# THE GHOSTS

SMITH, great writer of stories, drank; found it immortalised his pen;
Fused in his brain-pan, else a blank, heavens of glory now and then;
Gave him the magical genius touch; God-given power to gouge out, fling
Flat in your face a soul-thought — Bing!  Twiddle your heart-strings in his clutch.
"Bah!" said Smith, "let my body lie stripped to the buff in swinish shame,
If I can blaze in the radiant sky out of adoring stars my name.
Sober am I nonentitized; drunk am I more than half a god.
Well, let the flesh be sacrificed; spirit shall speak and shame the clod.
Who would not gladly, gladly give Life to do one thing that will live?"

Smith had a friend, we'll call him Brown; dearer than brothers were those two.
When in the wassail Smith would drown, Brown would rescue and pull him through.

# THE GHOSTS

When Brown was needful Smith would lend; so it fell
    as the years went by,
Each on the other would depend: then at the last Smith
    came to die.


There Brown sat in the sick man's room, still as a stone
    in his despair;
Smith bent on him his eyes of doom, shook back his lion
    mane of hair;
Said: " Is there one in my chosen line, writer of forth-
    right tales my peer?
Look in that little desk of mine; there is a package, bring
    it here.
Story of stories, gem of all; essence and triumph, key
    and clue;
Tale of a loving woman's fall; soul swept hell-ward, and
    God! it's true.
I was the man — Oh, yes, I've paid, paid with mighty and
    mordant pain.
Look! here's the masterpiece I've made out of my sin,
    my manhood slain.
Art supreme! yet the world would stare, know my mis-
    tress and blaze my shame.
I have a wife and daughter — there! take it and thrust
    it in the flame."

Brown answered: "Master, you have dipped pen in
    your heart, your phrases sear.

Ruthless, unflinching, you have stripped naked your soul
    and set it here.

Have I not loved you well and true? See! between us
    the shadows drift;

This bit of blood and tears means You — oh, let me
    have it, a parting gift.

Sacred I'll hold it, a trust divine; sacred your honour,
    her dark despair;

Never shall it see printed line: here, by the living God
    I swear."

Brown on a Bible laid his hand; Smith, great writer of
    stories, sighed:

"Comrade, I trust you, and understand. Keep my se-
    cret!" And so he died.


Smith was buried — up soared his sales; lured you his
    books in every store;

Exquisite, whimsy, heart-wrung tales; men devoured
    them and craved for more.

So when it slyly got about Brown had a posthumous man-
    uscript,

Jones, the publisher, sought him out, into his pocket
    deep he dipped.

# THE GHOSTS

"A thousand dollars?" Brown shook his head. "The
story is not for sale," he said.


Jones went away, then others came. Tempted and
taunted, Brown was true.
Guarded at friendship's shrine the fame of the unpub-
lished story grew and grew.
It's a long, long lane that has no end, but some lanes
end in the Potter's field;
Smith to Brown had been more than friend: patron, pro-
tector, spur and shield.
Poor, loving-wistful, dreamy Brown, long and lean, with
a smile askew,
Friendless he wandered up and down, gaunt as a wolf,
as hungry too.
Brown with his lilt of saucy rhyme, Brown with his tilt
of tender mirth
Garretless in the gloom and grime, singing his glad, mad
songs of earth:
So at last with a faith divine, down and down to the
Hunger-line.


There as he stood in a woeful plight, tears a-freeze on
his sharp cheek-bones,
Who should chance to behold his plight, but the publisher, the plethoric Jones;

Peered at him for a little while, held out a bill: "*Now,*
    will you sell?"

Brown scanned it with his twisted smile: "A thousand
    dollars! you go to hell!"

Brown enrolled in the homeless host, sleeping anywhere,
    anywhen;

Suffered, strove, became a ghost, slave of the lamp for
    other men;

For What's-his-name and So-and-so in the abyss his soul
    he stripped,

Yet in his want, his worst of woe, held he fast to the
    manuscript.

Then one day as he chewed his pen, half in hunger and
    half despair,

Creaked the door of his garret den; Dick, his brother,
    was standing there.

Down on the pallet bed he sank, ashen his face, his voice
    a wail:

"Save me, brother! I've robbed the bank; to-morrow
    it's ruin, capture, gaol.

Yet there's a chance: I could to-day pay back the money,
    save our name;

You have a manuscript, they say, worth a thousand —
    think, man! the shame. . . ."

Brown with his heart pain-pierced the while, with his
    stern, starved face, and his lips stone-pale,

Shuddered and smiled his twisted smile: " Brother, I
    guess you go to gaol."

While poor Brown in the leer of dawn wrestled with
    God for the sacred fire,
Came there a woman weak and wan, out of the mob, the
    murk, the mire;
Frail as a reed, a fellow ghost, weary with woe, with
    sorrowing;
Two pale souls in the legion lost; lo! Love bent with a
    tender wing,
Taught them a joy so deep, so true, it seemed that the
    whole-world fabric shook,
Thrilled and dissolved in radiant dew: then Brown made
    him a golden book,
Full of the faith that Life is good, that the earth is a
    dream divinely fair,
Lauding his gem of womanhood in many a lyric rich
    and rare;
Took it to Jones, who shook his head: " I will consider
    it," he said.

While he considered, Brown's wife lay clutched in the
    tentacles of pain;
Then came the doctor, grave and grey; spoke of decline,
    of nervous strain;

# THE GHOSTS

Hinted Egypt, the South of France — Brown with terror was tiger-gripped.

Where was the money? What the chance? Pitiful God! . . . the manuscript!

A thousand dollars! his only hope! he gazed and gazed at the garret wall. . . .

Reached at last for the envelope, turned to his wife and told her all.

Told of his friend, his promise true; told like his very heart would break:

"Oh, my dearest! what shall I do? shall I not sell it for your sake?"

Ghostlike she lay, as still as doom; turned to the wall her weary head;

Icy-cold in the pallid gloom, silent as death . . . at last she said:

"Do! my husband? Keep your vow! Guard his secret and let me die. . . .

Oh, my dear, I must tell you now — *the woman he loved and wronged was I;*

Darling! I haven't long to live: I never told you — forgive, forgive!"

For a long, long time Brown did not speak; sat bleak-browed in the wretched room;

Slowly a tear stole down his cheek, and he kissed her hand in the dismal gloom.

## THE GHOSTS

To break his oath, to brand her shame; his well-loved
    friend, his worshipped wife;
To keep his vow, to save her name, yet at the cost of
    what? Her life!
A moment's space did he hesitate, a moment of pain and
    dread and doubt,
Then he broke the seals, and, stern as fate, unfolded the
    sheets and spread them out. . . .
On his knees by her side he limply sank, peering amazed
    — *each page was blank*.


(For oh, the supremest of our art are the stories we do
    not dare to tell,
Locked in the silence of the heart, for the awful records
    of Heav'n and Hell.)


Yet those two in the silence there, seemed less weariful
    than before.
Hark! a step on the garret stair, a postman knocks at the
    flimsy door.
·' Registered letter!" Brown thrills with fear; opens,
    and reads, then bends above:
" Glorious tidings! Egypt, dear! The book is accepted
    — life and love."

## GOOD-BYE, LITTLE CABIN

O DEAR little cabin, I've loved you so long,
    And now I must bid you good-bye!
I've filled you with laughter, I've thrilled you with song,
And sometimes I've wished I could cry.
Your walls they have witnessed a weariful fight,
And rung to a won Waterloo:
But oh, in my triumph I'm dreary to-night —
Good-bye, little cabin, to you!

Your roof is bewhiskered, your floor is a-slant,
Your walls seem to sag and to swing;
I'm trying to find just your faults, but I can't —
You poor, tired, heart-broken old thing!
I've seen when you've been the best friend that I had,
Your light like a gem on the snow;
You're sort of a part of me — Gee! but I'm sad;
I hate, little cabin, to go.

Below your cracked window red raspberries climb;
A hornet's nest hangs from a beam;
Your rafters are scribbled with adage and rhyme,
And dimmed with tobacco and dream.

## GOOD-BYE, LITTLE CABIN

"Each day has its laugh," and "Don't worry, just
    work."
Such mottoes reproachfully shine.
Old calendars dangle — what memories lurk
About you, dear cabin of mine!

I hear the world-call and the clang of the fight;
I hear the hoarse cry of my kind;
Yet well do I know, as I quit you to-night,
It's Youth that I'm leaving behind.
And often I'll think of you, empty and black,
Moose antlers nailed over your door:
Oh, if I should perish my ghost will come back
To dwell in you, cabin, once more!

How cold, still and lonely, how weary you seem!
A last wistful look and I'll go.
Oh, will you remember the lad with his dream!
The lad that you comforted so.
The shadows enfold you, it's drawing to-night;
The evening star needles the sky:
And huh! but it's stinging and stabbing my sight —
God bless you, old cabin, good-bye!

## HEART O' THE NORTH

AND when I come to the dim trail-end,
    I who have been Life's rover,
This is all I would ask, my friend,
    Over and over and over:

A little space on a stony hill
    With never another near me,
Sky o' the North that's vast and still,
    With a single star to cheer me;

Star that gleams on a moss-grey stone
    Graven by those who love me —
There would I lie alone, alone,
    With a single pine above me;

Pine that the north wind whinneys through —
    Oh, I have been Life's lover!
But there I'd lie and listen to
    Eternity passing over.

# THE SCRIBE'S PRAYER

WHEN from my fumbling hand the tired pen
    falls,
And in the twilight weary droops my head;
While to my quiet heart a still voice calls,
Calls me to join my kindred of the Dead:
Grant that I may, O Lord, ere rest be mine,
Write to Thy praise one radiant, ringing line.

For all of worth that in this clay abides,
The leaping rapture and the ardent flame,
The hope, the high resolve, the faith that guides:
All, all is Thine, and liveth in Thy name:
Lord, have I dallied with the sacred fire!
Lord, have I trailed Thy glory in the mire!

E'en as a toper from the dram-shop reeling,
Sees in his garret's blackness, dazzling fair,
All that he might have been, and, heart-sick, kneel-
    ing,
Sobs in the passion of a vast despair:
So my ideal self haunts me alway —
When the accounting comes, how shall I pay?

# THE SCRIBE'S PRAYER

*For in the dark I grope, nor understand;*
*And in my heart fight selfishness and sin:*
*Yet, Lord, I do not seek Thy helping hand;*
*Rather let me my own salvation win:*
*Let me through strife and penitential pain*
*Onward and upward to the heights attain.*

*Yea, let me live my life, its meaning seek;*
*Bear myself fitly in the ringing fight;*
*Strive to be strong that I may aid the weak;*
*Dare to be true — O God! the Light, the Light!*
*Cometh the Dark so soon. I've mocked Thy Word,*
*Yet do I know Thy Love: have mercy, Lord. . . .*

**FINIS**